ARROWED

RESORT TO MURDER IV

AVERY DANIELS

Blazing Sword
Publishing Ltd.

Avery Daniels / Blazing Sword Publishing, Ltd.

Colorado Springs, CO. www.blazingswordpub.com

Publisher's note: This is a work of fiction. Names, characters, places, and incidents are products of the author's imagination or are used fictitiously. Locals and public names are sometimes used for atmospheric purposes. Any resemblance to actual people, living or dead, is entirely coincidental.

Cover art, layout, and design by Jess Smith / Inkblots Art

ARROWED/Avery Daniels 1st editions

 Created with Vellum

By each crime and every kindness, we birth our future.
    -David Mitchell

CHAPTER 1

The young woman at the registration desk looked up. "How may I help you?"

"Julienne LaMere and Mason Sheridan checking in." My smile was as weary as I felt. The five-hour drive to Santa Fe quickly became six and a half hours with all the road work on the highway. I blessed the air conditioner in the car for keeping us from melting into puddles in the record high New Mexico heat. It was late afternoon and one-hundred-one degrees in the shade.

I was thrilled to experience New Mexico, the forty-seventh state in the union, with its strong Spanish and Native American heritage. The splendor of a grand Hacienda entryway serving as the lobby surrounded me. The adobe walls were in shades of terra-cotta and warm ochre and the doorways were all arched, giving it a festive yet old world feel. Red clay tile floors glowed under the sleek modern lights. The lobby seating area, that surrounded a curved adobe fireplace, consisted of a couch and chairs with carved pine frames and vibrant fabric of southwest design in red, turquoise blue, and jade green with a matching area rug. Potted ferns of various types and heights were scattered throughout the lobby. It looked rustic and old Spanish style, but it was posh in its unique way. I adored it after all the Italian gilt decor at my home resort.

The young lady looked around before asking, "Where is Mr. Sheridan?"

I managed, "Parking the car" before he strode into the lobby of the Enchantment Canyon Resort with a confident air. The sight of him gave me jelly knees and a fluttering stomach.

The registration clerk's eyes widened when she saw Mason and followed him as he joined me. It was the usual reaction from most women when they first saw Mason. He had a model's good looks with intense hazel eyes framed by long lashes. His dark hair was shoulder length and fell in lush curls and waves that accentuated his cheekbones and strong chin sporting a five-o'clock shadow. It all gave him a dangerous aura that drew women like a magnet.

I was adjusting to the probability that this time away together, despite my having to work, would likely provide an opportunity for us to have intimate time. Which had me a tad bit anxious. Porsche, my best friend since high school who was much more experienced in dating, kept telling me that I didn't have to fret, just let things progress naturally. But I was worried somehow I would manage to not measure up and he would realize we weren't meant to be together. When it came to men, I was a smidgen insecure.

After tapping keys on her terminal, The clerk's brows furrowed, and she turned to the back counter and used the phone. Upon hanging up, she turned and said, "Please wait just a moment, I need to check something on your reservation."

I'm a Manager-in-training for the Colorado Springs Resort and its owner had recently purchased this body, mind, and spirit wellness resort outside Santa Fe. I was sent to train the staff on the owner's expectations, operating procedures, and the new software that linked this facility with the flagship resort in Colorado. Since my tab was being covered by the owner, I hoped she simply didn't understand the billing for my account. I didn't want to make her uncomfortable by jumping in to explain.

I began drumming my fingers on the hand carved reception desk when a middle aged woman with soft brown hair approached in a summery coral blazer and coordinating floral full skirt. "Ms. LaMere, I'd like to welcome you to Enchantment Canyon Resort. I'm Audrey, the Guest Services Manager. If there is anything I can do to get you settled, just let me know." She smiled warmly.

"Thank you Audrey, I appreciate the welcome." I tilted my head, "you look familiar --"

"We met at the Resort Management conference in Vail this last January. We were in a few of the workshops together." Her eyebrows danced.

Ah, we were foxhole compatriots. We were stuck at a conference in the middle of a record-breaking snowfall and dangerous blizzard in the Rocky Mountains with a killer in the resort. It's the sort of story most people don't believe when you tell them about it. I had assisted the detective investigating the deaths by passing along what gossip on motives I could uncover.

I introduced Audrey to Mason, and she took over checking us in. By the time we had our room key cards, I was looking forward to finding a Margarita and relaxing a bit. I spun around and bumped into a whisper thin woman waiting her turn behind me.

"Oh pardon me ma'am, I'm so sorry." I turned bright red from my blunder. Mason's hand was on my lower back to steady me. It flitted through my mind that this was a wellness getaway, so perhaps the woman was recovering from an illness to be so gaunt and down right boney. I needed to understand the clientele to adjust the training.

She smiled in return and in a reserved voice said, "Not a problem, dear."

Mason pushed the up arrow for the elevator. "I think we need to have a nice relaxing meal with a few drinks. Maybe sit in the pool to watch the sunset. Does that sound good to you?" Mason asked.

Down a hallway, a group of about twenty people filed out of a room and flooded the lobby. About half of them joined us at the elevator. The prior hush of the lobby was now filled with the noise of people talking over each other. I caught snippets from the people directly behind me and glanced at them.

"That was dry and boring, just like last year's kick-off. I need a scotch...." A woman said.

"Why do we go through this charade? Let's just wife swap and quit pretending this is for the company..." A man said.

"Connor, not everybody thinks like you. Some are here to learn and network..." A man replied.

"Don't pretend it isn't what happens at every business conference or convention." The tanned Connor replied in a clipped tone.

"Give it a rest Connor, it's mostly for Merritt to have a tax write off--" A woman said. I tucked that tidbit of information away. Merritt must be the head of this company.

"Who cares, we get to go to posh resorts and get tanned." Another man replied with a shrug of his shoulders.

Mason and I looked at each other. He took my hand and we made our way to the graceful stairway along the wall with intricate wrought iron balustrades.

From the sounds of their talk, it was a corporate retreat. You know the type where all the executives stay in luxury hotels and attend team building and company strategy meetings. But it sounded like this company had issues among its executives.

As we ascended the stairs, I looked down and saw a middle-aged man wearing an expensive white blazer, no tie, and blue jeans with a woman next to him taking notes. I guessed he was the leader of this pack, Merritt. In that brief look, I noticed several of the elevator group glared with evident scorn at him. Even the woman I had bumped into glanced over her shoulder at him with a frown.

Our room was a standard, no upgrade. It had a prominent rounded adobe fireplace in terracotta red, while the rest of the walls were a golden sand color. Around the fireplace were similar chairs as in the lobby. The rest of the room had brightly colored southwest fabric for the bedspread and curtains. We had a sliding door leading to a balcony furnished with a bistro style table and chairs. It was warm and inviting with the feel of cultural richness and I fell in love with it.

I sent out a group text with a photo of the room to my family and friends that we had arrived and were settling in. My cousin Felicia and friend Porsche teased me about time with Mason and not leaving the room. I got texts from my neighbors, a group of mature residents that kept tabs on Mason and I, they all were glad we arrived without incident. My father wanted me to call, but I replied I needed to get to the restaurant before it closed. He could be a bit over protective and I just wanted to relax.

Mason and I unpacked, freshened up, and were downstairs in record time. It was so good to move around after the drive. We strolled around the property to familiarize ourselves with the layout. The main building with lodging, restaurant and cafe, and both indoor or outdoor pools was in the center, to the left was the spa building and to right we found the tennis courts, volleyball sanded area, and trailheads to a few hiking trails that appeared to lead to a rocky hill behind the complex. The grounds had lush landscaping along the sidewalks with occasional park benches. This was a desert area, so the plants were various Palm bushes and trees, a number of flowering bushes, yucca, hardy red Bougainvillea, whispery Mexican Feather Grass, and other ornamental grasses. It was serene and comforting.

We were hungry and found the Enchantée restaurant easily. It had the same stucco walls but in a turquoise green and the southwestern archways, but the ceiling had large rough wood planks crossing it for a more rustic atmosphere. Classical Spanish guitar played and the white linen table cloths gave a sophisticated touch.

The menu had few Mexican food options along with American dishes made in a healthy reimagining in some cases, plus gluten-free, low calorie, and low carb options. We decided on an appetizer of cactus fries, I ordered the Chicken Mole and Mason decided on the meat-stuffed Poblanos with Cilantro-Lime sauce and Mock-Margaritas for both. They didn't list alcoholic beverages on the menu. Mason whispered he would pick up some wine and mixed drink ingredients for our room tomorrow.

When our drinks arrived, Mason raised his glass, "Ma bichette, you are beautiful tonight. I'm so glad to have this time away with you." He still called me his little doe. His eyes had a heat that burned through me, and I took a few gulps of my drink to cool my cheeks. Oh my, he sure could singe me with that consuming gaze.

My voice came out stronger than I expected when I

answered, "Thank you for making the time to join me. I know you had the poker tournament, but we needed the time alone..." I let myself swim in his hazel eyes.

Mason plays high stakes poker and wins regularly. He is also building his reputation as a professional photographer. In his past, he was Marine Special Forces, sniper classified, black belt fourth degree in Marine Corps martial arts and black belt fifth degree in TaeKwonDo. But he did all that to satisfy his demanding father, an Air Force General.

When we met, and up until a few months ago, he would pose as the boyfriend photographer for Hollywood and recording celebrities while actually being their bodyguard for a few weeks. This got his name out as a photographer and allowed the celebrities to keep it quiet that they had a hostile ex or a stalker. He was gone a lot while I saw celebrity gossip of him that left me wondering what was happening with all the beautiful women.

We had broken up for a few months until working the issues out. He only does bodyguard work for men and openly as hired muscle now, so I don't have to be reading about him in celebrity gossip magazines. But getting time without my cousins, or Aunt Regina and Uncle Lars, or Mason's sister Marissa intruding was a serious challenge.

He took my hand and kissed the back, never taking

his eyes from mine. *Gulp.* "I jumped at the chance for us to get away, without our families interrupting every romantic moment."

We'd had several close calls. Once with my cousin Felicia when we were getting amorous on my couch and another time with Marissa walking in on us at Mason's. Something was always spoiling the moment. Maybe that was part of my anxiety about our upcoming alone time, the anticipation after several disruptions!

Our food arrived and was perfect. With each bite and sip of Margarita I relaxed. I had tonight with Mason before starting tomorrow with the employees. I could feel the possibilities with each smoldering glance from Mason that reached down to my toes.

We both enjoy watching people, and the corporate meeting folks in the restaurant provided subtle drama. We had plenty to entertain us with this bunch. Close to our table was the man I believed was the top dog, *Merritt,* with an exotic beauty that must be his wife. Up close, he was tanned with a still trim physique but signs of thickening around his middle sneaking up on him. His companion was easily twenty years younger, almond eyes, long legged, pushed up cleavage on display, and olive complexion. She was the closest to a modern Sophia Loren I had ever witnessed. But they seemed to ignore each other.

Mason looked at me and said, "The tension is thick in here. These executives seem pretty scandalous."

I leaned closer and whispered, "I think the guy in the white blazer is their boss, Merritt. He and his wife seem far more interested in others than each other."

"She seems to be making eyes at that man across the room there." He waved his fork to *Connor* from the group at the elevator earlier who mentioned wife swapping. "I need a cigarette after watching those two," he finished. He didn't even smoke.

But I understood. "Well, her hubby is just as bad. I think he is sexting with that man's wife two tables to his left," I whispered.

We watched as Merritt would text on his phone and then watch for a reaction from the woman at the other table. She read the text and dipped her finger in her wine glass and stroked it down her cleavage and suggestively licked her lips while looking at him.

We grew tired of the soap opera around us and talked about Mason's plans for some photography outings while I worked with the resort staff. He wanted to get photos of the sandstone crags of Abiquiu geological formation at sunrise, unique desert cactus, and a desert lightning storm, if nature cooperated. Often he had to wait patiently for the perfect conditions to get that stunning photo like you see in ads or in calendars. He would be busy during the days since Abuquiu was a few hour drive one way. That worked out fine since I would be training during the day and we would at least have the evenings together.

We finished dinner and made our way to the lounge for some dancing nice and slow in each other's arms. I had regained some energy from dinner and relaxing. I may have given a sigh of contentment, swaying to the live music with my head against his shoulder. It was so right, so perfect in his strong arms with his cologne of leather, patchouli, and sandalwood swirled together, enveloping me.

After several songs passed with us oblivious to any other living being, just wrapped up in each other, we stepped outside to stroll in the golden glow of a nearly full moon before heading to our room. We walked hand-in-hand until we were surrounded by the land-scaping and the shimmering moonlight through the trees. Mason stopped and wrapped his muscular arms around me.

"I am so grateful for you in my life. I hope I never take you for granted or forget to tell you how important you are to me." He kissed me, sweet and slow. He drew me closer, and the kiss deepened. I slid my hands up his chest and around his neck. My head and heart were spinning.

I felt something brush my foot. *Don't spoil the moment LaMere, focus on the kiss.* I succumbed to the kiss again. It had probably been a rabbit startled out of its hiding spot, right?

After another moment of blissful necking, my foot was brushed again before a hand - yes, a hand - grasped my left ankle. I let out a yelp and jumped. Mason pulled back and looked into my eyes.

"A hand just latched onto my ankle!" I don't know why I was whispering, whoever owned the hand knew they had me in their grasp.

We shifted and looked down to see an arm in a soiled white blazer reaching out from the bushes along the pathway. The blazer glowed eerily in the moonlight. The hand at the end of the arm was attached to my ankle. I shook my foot, and the hand slipped away. Mason released me, took a hold of the arm, and dragged Merritt, face up, out of the foliage. He had an ancient looking arrow of wood protruding from his chest and blood drenched his shirt. Mason bent down and placed two fingers to his throat.

Merritt's head twitched, and he breathed out a few words, "It's the curse. I can't believe it, the curse got me." And he seemed to deflate like a balloon leaking air until he went flat, like the animating force had left him.

What curse is he talking about? Oh my, I may never kiss again.

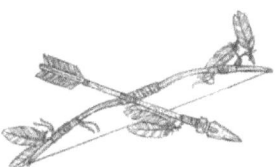

$\mathcal{T}$he peaceful, idyllic, and romantic garden was now overrun with local police. The glow of the moon was replaced by flashlights and resort flood lights. The gentle serenade of crickets gave way to police chatter on comm links. Mason and I were separated and questioned multiple times. I was currently not being interrogated, so Audrey joined me as well as another resort employee.

"What happened? I saw them take a body away." Audrey asked. Her eyebrows were furrowed and her voice was a tad high.

I went over what I had told the police multiple times but didn't share the gory details. I had it down to a streamlined report.

"Yes, Merritt wore the white blazer today. How horrible to find him dying, Julienne. Oh, this is simply terrible. This has never happened before. He seemed healthy and active to just die." Audrey said, concern and stress evident.

I kept my mouth shut. No time to share this was murder, and it wasn't my first resort murder at that. Last fall my home resort had a murder of a celebrity pastor and since then I had been on the periphery of a few others. I even assisted the police a teensy weensy bit, too. That's why I am now cross-training in security as well as management.

I realized I didn't know who the gentleman with Audrey was since we had skipped introductions. I held out my hand, "I'm Julienne, and your name is…?"

"Jonathon, the general manager. I wanted to assure you nothing like this has happened before. Please emphasize to Mr. Carlton that we remain a reputable establishment." He delivered his speech with stiff efficiency, as if he had practiced it in front of a mirror. I could sympathize and would probably be sweating if I were in his shoes with a new owner just taking over.

"I will certainly pass that along, sir. This will prove to be unrelated to the resort, I'm sure." At least, I hoped that was the case.

Audrey looked embarrassed she had forgotten to introduce him. I smiled to reassure her. Jonathon excused himself and left, saying he needed to keep the reporters away.

"Can I ask a question?" I said.

"Of course, what is it?" Audrey took a breath like she expected I would critique her or the resort.

"Just before Mr. Merritt," I cleared my throat, "before he lost consciousness, he said the curse got him. Do you have any idea what curse he was referring to?" Just as I asked, Mason joined us and slipped his arm around me from the side. His strength, warm presence, and spicy cologne were comforting.

"I imagine he is referring to the local legend of a vengeful brave. That is the only thing that comes to my mind. We have a plaque with the story along with a display of an ancient Native American bow and arrow that some believe belonged to the young brave. It's in the library we have for guests."

My curiosity was definitely engaged. I planned on stopping in the library very soon and checking it out. But while I had Audrey here, I wanted to know who the other players in this drama were.

"We figured there was a corporate retreat going on from the looks of it." Mason got the ball rolling.

Audrey shook her head yes, "For the last decade the Howell Venture Capital Firm has had their annual executive retreat here. They just had their kickoff earlier today."

She nudged her chin towards a small group of guests watching the police activity and whispering among themselves, "There are a few of them. The thin guy in his forties with premature balding is the Chief Financial Officer Preston Richards. The guy next to him in the snug polo shirt and pants is Senior Vice President Connor Gallard, and the woman holding on to Connor is the deceased's wife, Margaux. Behind them the tall blond with her husband is Barbara Dolin, the Human Resources Director. Senior VP of Acquisitions, David Raptor, is the brown haired guy with the fake tan."

Margaux was the exotic beauty I noticed with Merritt in the dining room earlier. From the familiarity between Margaux and Connor, I suspected they knew each other a tad too well. Margaux reached up and rubbed a smear of lipstick off his neck with her thumb. Yep.

"Who do you think will assume Merritt's job?" Mason asked Audrey.

She shrugged, "I've heard some gossip that Connor has been gunning to take over. But that was overheard in the lounge, so there is no telling how accurate it is."

I also noticed the thin lady I had backed into earlier, she was wearing dark slacks and blouse like she had a night out. She was just joining the group and seemed agitated. "What about that lady just arriving? Who is she?"

"Blair something. She seems familiar to me, but I can't place it." She shook her head.

I glanced over to "Blair something," we looked at each other and she nodded her head in acknowledgment. She seemed tired and sad to me.

A police detective joined us and Audrey excused herself.

The detective was big and bulky, like a football linebacker waiting to tackle a defensive end. "I'm Detective Sullivan. Miss LaMere, Mr. Sheridan, we have your statements so you are free to return to the resort. Forensics will be out here for a few hours yet, but we will be discouraging the curious from hanging about the area any longer. I'll be in touch if there is anything further." As he finished, large flood lights atop stands switched on and drowned the lush garden landscaping with harsh LED illumination that stripped the colors from the foliage, making it seem clinical and impersonal.

Detective Sullivan handed his card to us and I took it, "Call me if you think of anything else from this evening. Try to get some sleep." He turned and walked to the technicians in full hooded jumpsuits with booties and gloves.

Mason and I turned and walked towards to the main building of the resort

"We need to find the guest library. There is a plaque I really want to see on display there." I said.

"And here I was worried the close encounter with another dead body would have you traumatized," Mason chuckled. "So, we are looking into the curse already."

"Yes, just curious." I tried to be nonchalant, but I don't think he believed my facade since he winked.

We asked at the desk and were directed down a side hall off the lobby. The entrance was an arch with a matching arched rustic wooden door. The guest library had a cozy feel with a gas fireplace, six-foot rustic bookshelves, and several leather chairs sprinkled around. Tucked away in one open corner was the display case, with a metal plaque on the wall behind it.

Legend of A Brave's Revenge

THERE WAS open war between the Apache and the government that wanted to settle what is now New Mexico, Arizona, and Texas. Whether it was soldiers or a band of drunk white settlers depends on which version you hear, but a group of about ten men abducted three young Apache maidens. Some say it was Cochise while others say it was Geronimo, but many elders believe it was a young brave who had pledged his heart to one of the maidens. He took only two warriors with him to rescue the maidens. The three braves did a sacred ceremony before leaving and swore vengeance *before the Great Spirit for every hurt and violation to the three maidens.*

They set out knowing they would give their lives to free the maidens, but knew they would take as many of the abductors with them to the spirit land. By nightfall they had the abductors camp surrounded. They mimicked an owl hooting to alert the maidens that death was in the camp. Within a short quarter of an hour the men were tied up, and the maidens told of their abuse by each man's hands. Each man then received punishment in the same manner as they had doled out to the maidens.

By sunrise the ten men were left tied up for the Great Spirit to finish with them and they returned the maidens never divulging what they had endured. The warrior braves told their people the girls had been rescued before they could be violated in order to save their honor. It is said that the young warrior brave who led the raid wanders the hills here, and if you hear an owl that keeps hooting, then vengeance is about to be delivered to an evil man. Here is displayed what many believe is the bow and arrow the brave took with him as a symbol to all who have done evil, that their reward will be swift like an arrow to the heart.

THE STORY WAS sad and serious, but I was more disturbed by the empty display case with a hole in one end. Mason left to inform Detective Sullivan that perhaps the old arrow in Merritt's chest had been the one belonging in the display. I turned on my phone's flashlight and looked all over the floor and around the display, but found no small clues. I turned off the flashlight feature just as the detective entered the library with Mason. Mason was back by my side with his arm around me for support again.

The detective looked at the case and the plaque before turning to me. "You think this was a robbery and not something simple like removal for routine preservation efforts?"

"I told you that Merritt Howell said the curse killed him. I asked a staff member what that might mean, and they could only think of this legend and directed me here. The staff member never mentioned it being gone or unavailable." I withheld Audrey's name at this point in case it was nothing. I knew what it was like to have a Detective misread intentions. "If he was killed with an arrow from the Brave's Revenge Legend display, then he would think the curse had gotten him."

Detective Sullivan shook his head, his dark hair showing the glimmer of grey hairs in the light. "It may be linked, or it may not. Thank you for alerting me right away."

Detective Sullivan exited the guest library as Audrey walked in with a frown. "I hope that wasn't bad news?" She twisted her hands.

How to break this latest discovery? I guess just ripping off the bandage was the best approach.

"I hate to be the one to tell you, but I came to see the plaque you told me about and found your display had been looted."

Her mouth fell open and a look of disbelief dominated her face. She looked at the display sitting empty but didn't move. I took her arm and led her to one of the red leather chairs and told her to sit. She moved as if in shock, her eyes never leaving the display case.

"How? Why?"

Mason stepped up, "Perhaps a little drink to revive her is in order. I'll bring something."

Audrey sat staring at the display case until Mason returned and knelt in front of her with iced tea. "Audrey, please take a drink now." She finally looked into his eyes, then down to his extended hand with the drink. She grabbed the glass and drank it in several gulps like she was downing the only water after days in the desert. She shook her head and let out a breath.

Mason took the empty glass back.

Audrey was sufficiently revived and now began to talk directly to Mason, "I don't know what came over me. I've just never had to deal with murder before and then to have an insignificant little relic stolen too. What's going on? We are a peaceful resort. Sure, we have the occasional petty theft of money from a purse left unattended or loud guests, but murder! I don't know what to make of this." She was shaking her head through her speech.

"Were the bow and arrow on display worth much?" I said. She barely glanced my way before looking into Mason's eyes again like they were a life preserver and she was afloat in the ocean. I didn't mind, I got lost in his eyes all the time and she'd had a shock.

She swallowed, "No, they were more a novelty. But we were honored to have them on loan from the local Indigeonous tribe. They believe the legend and felt the items were the brave's, but local historians and an archeologist or two didn't feel they were of much historical significance."

She jumped up, "I must lock this room up for now, in case the police need to have their team look it over." We stepped out into the hall. After locking up the big rustic doors, she walked off muttering, "I just don't understand."

We turned to go to our room, romantic mood and libido sufficiently killed.

CHAPTER 3

*L*ast night had been a bust for romance after being grabbed by a dying man. I hated getting up the next morning since it took so long for me to get to sleep. I kept thinking my ankle was touched or grabbed. That would take a while to get over.

I opted to skip breakfast after a few cups of coffee in the room. I stayed in my room answering calls from dad, who lived in Florida, my Aunt Regina and Uncle Lars back home in Colorado Springs, and my best friend Porsche. *I'm fine, thanks. Yes, I discovered the body - again! No, I'm not getting involved.* Once again I had to stress to dear old Dad that I wouldn't quit my dream job, nor was I going to get married and stay safely at home. I didn't want to leave my brightly colored oasis, but I was tired of the calls and I had training to conduct.

The plan was to train the staff on the new software that the owner, Chandler Carlton, was switching them over to in the next few weeks. I would have Audrey, Jonathon, and Carlos from Security, and the head of Maintenance Barry to go over the management side of the program. Tomorrow I would have several from the front desk and housekeeping to instruct, and they would help tutor the rest of the staff.

Meanwhile, Mason was going to get some scouting done for optimal sites to get the photos he desired. He would consider different times of day for the photos, but today was identifying spots that had the most potential. Mason packed up his extra water, granola, and energy bars, along with hats, sunglasses, and sunscreen in a backpack. He drove off as I made my way to the front desk where I was to meet Audrey.

The executive retreat participants were making their way down the hall to the meeting rooms. They were unusually quiet and reserved compared to my first impression of them yesterday. The murder of your CEO would have that effect. I noticed Connor greeting everyone as though he had already stepped into Merritt's place as CEO.

Audrey came rushing up from the other direction,

"I'm sorry to make you wait. This morning has been one phone call after another."

"Can you arrange for security to handle the press when they descend, and they will, once the initial news is out that Merritt Howell died here?"

She paled visibly and swallowed, "Do you really think - ?"

I interrupted her, "I know they will, and they will be relentless. This I know from experience."

She swallowed again, then walked to the front desk and made a phone call.

Before she had even hung up, a news van pulled up to the doors and a man with a microphone jumped out with a cameraman close behind him. They burst through the doors with the camera recording.

I intercepted them with my hand out in the universal stop signal, "No press allowed in the Resort without special invitation. Please leave now or we will call the police and press charges." I hoped I sounded far more sure of myself than I felt. *Where was Carlos and security?*

He thrust a microphone in my face, "Who discovered the body of Mr. Howell?" The microphone in my face was intimidating.

But I wasn't going to tell them! "I said you must leave right now. That's the only comment you'll get." I crossed my arms and stood in his way. Audrey and the two front desk agents joined me, forming a barricade in their way.

The reporter kept asking questions, but we remained silent. He tried to make an end run around us and we scrambled to block him. It would have been funny if it weren't a matter of the resort's survival because of a high-profile death on the premises.

Finally, Carlos arrived with security, "I've called the police on your trespassing. I suggest you leave before they get here." The reporter turned and walked out. But I had a feeling this wasn't over.

Just as the van pulled away, another pulled up and another reporter, this one a woman from a national news station, was talking to the camera as she walked into the lobby.

Carlos waved us away as he and his two men confronted her with their arms crossed, blocking her way. We had to come up with a better strategy than this, and fast. Salacious news was most reporter's relentless craving, their drug of choice.

"Who handles your publicity or marketing?" I asked Audrey.

"Jonathon has always taken care of all that."

"Ms. LaMere, Chandler Carlton is calling for you." One of the front desk people announced. *Great, my first big assignment and I'm blowing it before I even start.* Chandler Carlton was the owner of the resort I work for and the new owner of Enchantment Canyon Resort.

"Mr. Carlton, I can guess why you are calling." I wanted to at least appear on top of things.

"LaMere, I've seen a news report about a murder at Enchantment Canyon. I will not comment on how many murders you have been near over the last year," he took a weary breath while I let one out. "I'm not going to wonder why you seem to always be involved or around suspicious deaths, I'm going to be grateful that you weren't a suspect this time. But LaMere, I'm going to insist that you deal with this, since you are probably the expert in residence on murders. Make the media attention go away! Keep me updated." He hung up.

I slowly replaced the phone handset into the cradle. That went better than I expected, all things considered. I squared my shoulders and nodded my head. Okay, I could do this. Right?

Audrey was next to me in seconds of hanging up. "How bad?" She asked, her eyebrows bunched together and worry flooded her eyes.

"He wants me to make the media's attention go away. So, we need to do damage control." Audrey swallowed.

After fifteen minutes of convincing Jonathan that we needed a better strategy than praying it goes away, it took another fifteen minutes to convince him to hire a professional public relations expert. We found an excellent company in Santa Fe and arranged to meet with them in a few hours.

Meanwhile, my training of the management personnel on the new software was delayed until this afternoon. I wasn't happy with the delay and felt pressure to juggle two major tasks, neither of which were likely to be done well. I strolled to the lobby to check their progress and found Carlos at the door. I was just feeling we might have gotten a handle on the newshound invasion when the skinny woman I nearly backed into yesterday at check-in dashed up to me.

"Dear, you work here or something, don't you?" She was flustered and twisted her hands.

"Close enough, what can I do for you, miss…?"

"I'm Blair Palmer. I just thought somebody should know, I think a reporter is sneaking in from the back area. I saw two men, one with a camera. This way." She turned and sped down a hallway, surprising me. That'll teach me to judge a person by their appearance. She wasn't as frail or brittle as she appeared.

I shrugged and followed her to a floor to ceiling plate-glass window overlooking the outdoor pool and winding garden path that ends at a hiking trail into a rocky crag. There were two men huffing and puffing as they left the trail and stepped onto resort property. One hefted a television camera on his shoulder. I glanced around for a door and she pointed further down the wall of glass.

I charged off at a run like a bull after a red cape, grateful I had worn my practical comfy shoes. I hit the panic bar on the exit door at full speed and tore past the pool where three people were swimming laps. *I am getting my exercise for today.*

I rounded a bend in the landscaped garden path and plowed into the two men. I shook off my surprise and crossed my arms, fixing them with a glare. I was going for intimidating, but both men were around six foot, if not taller, and my slight five-five height was underwhelming.

"Reporters aren't allowed on the premises. You know that or you wouldn't be sneaking around. Now get off the property." My voice didn't squeak or squawk, I'm proud to say.

"Look at the itty bitty Chihuahua yapping away." The lead man without the camera on his shoulder said. Gee, did his juvenile attitude show on camera?

A short joke, really? I took offense for every small-in-stature being. I clenched my teeth and took my cell phone from my pocket and took a few photos of them. "Smile for the mug shot, guys." I then switched to video. "I've informed you that you must leave the property. What station are you with so our attorney can contact your boss?" I didn't have a clue if this was attorney territory, but maybe they wouldn't either. If they were going to call me a chihuahua, then I was going to emulate the little canine terrors with feisty attitudes.

Reporter-guy chuckled, "You can't expect to keep us from reporting this. The more you keep us out, the more reporters want to get the scoop." He was only partially correct in that, the more we kept them out the more we retained our guests.

"We will be providing an official statement, and if you give us time to put together a press meeting, we could answer questions. But every time we have to chase one of you down, we can't get to a press conference." I held the phone up a little higher, "Now which competing news channel do you want getting the footage of you being arrested for trespassing?" *See me be feisty!*

Blair trotted up with her phone to her ear, "The police are on the way, I'm staying on the phone with dispatch." She leveled a nasty glare at the reporter and cameraman.

"This isn't over." The reporter spit out and turned to go back the way he had come.

Blair and I followed them to make sure they were getting off the property. We stood at the base of the rocky crag where the trail began and waited until they were out of sight to go back.

"Thanks for calling the police, I should go explain when they get here." I said.

"Oh, I just pretended to call. I still had to push dial before the call went through. I just thought it would get them on their way." She smiled at me and her face transformed into a lovely lady. I hadn't noticed before how sad she had appeared until she lit up with mischief.

"You are tricky, lady. Good idea, though." She beamed from my praise.

I trudged back to see how the defenses at the front entrance were holding up. It wasn't even eleven o'clock yet, but I felt like I had spent the day dealing with reporters.

At the lobby and reception, one of Carlos' security people, a lady this time, was turning away a reporter. Who the heck was Merritt Howell to make his death such a big deal?

My cell phone began vibrating for an incoming call. I fished it out of my blazer pocket, my neighbor Delores. I live in a townhome community with more mature neighbors. Delores was in her late sixties and was no doubt calling for the gossip on the murder. I answered.

"Julie darling, *another* murder? Tell me everything." Delores said with a bit too much glee in her voice.

"I'm in the middle of defending the resort from

hordes of invading reporters, Delores." Only a slight exaggeration. After all, I was here to work, not chat on the phone.

"I'll make it quick then. What can I do to assist dear? You know I'm always here to help you out." Her tone was serious, but eager.

"Actually, can you research who this Merritt Howell was for me? There seems to be so much interest in his death. That would help me." I knew she would snatch this up, and she was proficient in internet research. I was just curious, that's all. I wouldn't get involved. Getting control of the situation was far different from sleuthing.

"I'm on it, dear. I'll find out everything from his net worth to his favorite drink and boxers or briefs. By the way, get lucky with Mason?" Yep, some things never change.

"Thank you for the research help. As for Mason and I, it's none of your business, deary." I didn't want our love life the topic of gossip back home. Who was I kidding, it already was most likely.

Audrey scurried up to me as soon as I hung up with Delores. "Can we do the management training after lunch, say 1:30? I am inundated with phone calls. That PR person said she would have our state-ment released by then and hopefully things will settle down after that." Her eyebrows were bunched together and her perfectly coiffed honey blond hair was disheveled.

"Absolutely. I will grab some lunch and then meet you in Jonathan's office." He had the largest office so that everyone could fit to see his monitor. Not optimal, but workable for training on the management side of the software. "When is the press conference?"

"She said she would arrange it for late afternoon so the reporters would be there in time for the evening news deadlines. Where should we hold that?" She asked.

"Show off the resort. Where do you have any weddings?"

"Oh, we don't really do weddings with our health and wellness specialty."

I asked to see their marketing brochures, and she brought me to her office. Out of a desk drawer, she handed me a trifold full-color brochure that was easy to mail. I looked it over, then pointed to a photo from inside the resort with an amazing view of the grounds. "This is where you want the press conference, so the amazing grounds are highlighted. Might as well put our best foot forward."

"That's a pilates and yoga room in the spa. It might be small depending on how many reporters and cameramen show up." She fretted.

"Then you be sure that the national news organizations are in the room and locals are to the back or outside. If we are getting national negative attention, we need the view to offset." She nodded her understanding, and I left.

I made my way into the Canyon Cafe on site, hoping to grab a quick sandwich. The cafe went for light and airy, so the walls were a soft sand color with white and turquoise accents. The lighting was bright and nature sounds replaced piped in music. The tables, natural pine without tablecloths, were spread out. Blair waved for me to join her at her table next to a large picture window. It would seem rude if I didn't at least chat with her for a moment. After all, she helped me block the reporter from getting any further onto the property.

"Are you sure you want me to intrude on your mealtime?" I asked when I walked over to her table that looked out the window onto the labyrinth constructed with waist-high shrubs.

She assured me I was welcome. After I placed my order of a very healthy sandwich on multigrain bread with freshly made soup, I settled back in my chair.

"What are they doing?" I asked about a group of people gathered around a man at the entrance to the labyrinth. He was handing each person a nice digital camera with a fancy lens.

"Oh, that is for the photography hike. I've been on

it before, years ago, and it is a wonderful activity." She was pushing the remnants of her carrots around on her plate.

"So you're a return customer. That says a lot about this resort."

"Oh my, yes. My late husband and I stayed here often. We probably came here five or so times before he got sick." Her sad expression was back, but now I understood why. She was probably still grieving.

"My condolences on your loss, Blair." I wasn't sure what else to say. "Did you do the photo hike when you stayed before?"

"Yes, I did. It is a pleasant hike, and it's surprising how much beauty there is in the desert that you don't expect."

I glanced out the window in time to witness the group follow the guide out of site. Everyone seemed in high spirits and unconcerned about the death last night, which was a good sign.

We chatted intermittently as I devoured my sandwich. She was pleasant company, and I found myself liking her quickly. I usually took a while to warm up to new people.

I checked my watch and excused myself. I made my way to Jonathan's office and prepared for a back-breaking afternoon of leaning over and directing each person how to navigate the software. The business offices were all interior so there weren't any windows and although Jonathon's was a little larger than the others, it was a tight squeeze with us all packed in. The company computer people were waiting for me to train everyone before they officially replaced the old software with the new and migrated their existing files over.

I pulled up the website where they could practice on Jonathan's computer and began walking Audrey through the management side of the software. Audrey was going to be the key person in residence to help the others, so I wanted to start with her as the others watched. Then I would give each a turn in the seat and have them do a few tasks for practice.

After a rushed three and a half hours and only one bathroom break, I finished the first session with them and handed out their homework sheets with the web address and their own logins. I would visit each person tomorrow in their offices and go through some one-on-one training. I handed out the owner's general guide-lines and procedures that he wanted integrated into their employee handbooks for them to peruse and get back to me with questions.

I was ready to leave when Jonathan stopped every-one. "I need a few moments of all your time."

He was probably going to give a pep talk and go over procedures concerning Merritt Howell's murder.

"I spoke with Mr. Chandler Carlton earlier today."

He made eye contact with each of us. I swallowed. Uh oh, I didn't like the sound of this. "Apparently Julienne is also trained in security and has investigated murders before. He would like her to coordinate with Carlos and the rest of the staff to conduct our own internal investigation of Howell's murder."

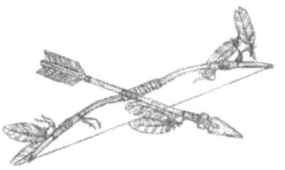

CHAPTER 4

*C*rap, crap, crap! How could Mr. Carlton do that to me? He made it sound like I was trained in investigating murders. I'm not trained. Breathe. Deep breaths!

The already cramped room felt like it was closing in on me. I really wish Mr. Carlton had discussed this with me first!

I had started cross training with security about three months ago, but I was very aware I'm not qualified for this. And as for my helping in a few murder investigations, I kept my eyes and ears open and reported back to the police. It wasn't the same as a trained homicide detective. I was fully aware of that fact.

Jonathan continued, oblivious to my distress, "I have already discussed this with Carlos and we will

assist Julienne in any way we can to get this behind us."
Everyone was nodding their agreement.

"I'm not really-"

"No need to be modest." Jonathan interjected.

Carlos jumped in, "All the staff has been informed
to cooperate with you in anything you ask." His expression was open and earnest.

The last thing I wanted was to be the outsider
taking over and causing resentment. But there was one
thing…

"I have found it particularly helpful before to have
the staff listen to the guests for gossip about the
murder." I held up my hand, "It isn't savory, but it
proves informative to know what they will tell another
guest but would never mention to the police. If we
could have a trustworthy employee be the point person
to gather all reports from the staff, everyone from the
maids to maintenance and landscaping. That person
can meet with me once or twice a day to deliver the
scuttlebutt. It's like Sherlock Holmes and his Baker
Street Irregulars."

They looked skeptical, glanced between one
another, then nodded.

I had found when I was snowbound with a killer six
months ago that gossip proved pretty effective in uncov-
ering motives quickly.

Carlos cleared his throat, "We were hoping for a

more direct approach. Perhaps more like Hercule Poirot." He seemed pleased to come up with an alternate literary example. "Anybody you would like to question, we can ask to my office and you could talk with them in private."

Oh boy, this was getting out of hand. I wanted to avoid overtly questioning anyone.

"I have found that people are more forthcoming if they don't think they are being interrogated. I'll try to encourage a conversation with people of interest without seeming to question them first. It's best to keep in mind that the killer probably won't enjoy being questioned, so stealth is preferable."

Everyone nodded at that. Okay, so far so good.

They discussed which employee should gather any "news" from others and coordinate with me. They settled on a maid named Graciella and promised to arrange for her to meet with me.

I couldn't wait to escape from that office, but Jonathon, Audrey, and I had the press conference to go to now.

We walked together over to the spa building that also had the pilates room where the press conference was being held. We were about thirty minutes early and maintenance had set up the space with four rows of folding chairs and a portable lectern at the front. The view through the wall of glass was idyllic and showered light into the room that I hoped offset the dissecting of the murder. The publicist joined us and handed us copies of the brief statement we were to make. We read it over and made minimal tweaks. Just before we were to start, Detective Sullivan joined us.

The space filled up fast and there were several left standing outside the door. A few cable news channels had sent reporters as well as the regular national and local channels being represented. Reporters were in the seats while cameramen were along the walls. The one thing I hadn't anticipated was with all the extra bodies crammed into the space, it became warm and stuffy.

We started exactly on time and Jonathon read the statement with a stiff back and never made eye contact. I could feel his tension in every rushed word and wooden movement. He stopped abruptly and motioned for Detective Sullivan to take over. The shifting in seats, texting, fanning themselves, and general movement ceased.

"Thank you all for being here. At this point, the Santa Fe Police Department is just beginning the investigation after spending the night collecting any evidence available. In the next few days, we will focus on identifying any persons of interest and questioning them as quickly as possible. The Executives of Howell Venture Capital have pledged full cooperation in the pursuit of the person or persons who killed Mr. Howell." Detective Sullivan spoke with confidence and authority. He continued on that the weapon at this point is believed to be a handmade wooden arrow. Tests were being run to confirm that. The Detective provided a phone number to call if anybody had information.

There were only a few questions, and the answers were all the same. *We don't have any further information at this point to answer sufficiently.* We wrapped up in twenty minutes once the reporters were done asking the same question in different ways and taking photos. Overall, I thought it went well. It wasn't the sort of activity that Jonathan's stage fright would be a detriment.

I excused myself since there wasn't anything further I could help with and pushed through the throng of media milling about or recording a reporter outside. Relieved to reach the lobby where resort security kept reporters out, I plopped into one of the chairs around the dormant fireplace. It felt like the last twenty-four hours had been a sluggish race to nowhere.

My phone buzzed. Mason had returned from his photography scouting of the day and asked if I wanted to meet him at the restaurant for dinner or did I need to freshen up first. I texted back to meet me in the Enchantée restaurant and I needed a drink.

As usual, the sight of Mason walking towards me as I waited outside the restaurant was surreal. We had gone through significant relationship issues and worked them out. I knew he wanted to be with me and would make the effort for the long term. I had to pinch myself. He wore comfortable light gray slacks and a mint green polo shirt that turned several women's heads.

It was the same restaurant as last night and I found the classical guitar music and turquoise walls comforting, like another world from the claustrophobic office. We got seated at our table and settled with large iced tea for him and a mock Margarita for me. He slipped a shot of tequila in my drink from a travel size bottle he brought in his pocket. Thank goodness he remembered to pick up even a little something for mixed drinks.

Mason's hazel eyes sparkled as he told me about the great locations he found for some sunrise photos with impressive rock formations and a few other spots with interesting vegetation he could incorporate. He was an early morning person after his stint in the Marines, so sunrise photos weren't a hardship for him. He planned on selling the photos to a calendar company he had worked with before, and they had already promised to look at what he brought back.

He winked at me, "Thanks for letting me talk so much. Now, tell me about your day and don't leave anything out."

I shared everything between sips of my Margarita. I lowered my voice when I got to the part about Chandler Carlton setting me up to investigate for the resort.

"I can't believe he would do such a thing? That puts you at risk." His eyes filled with worry.

"I got them to tone it down, gather what the staff overhears, and let me gossip with some people. I'm hoping that'll satisfy them. If I come across anything worth the trouble, I'll call the detective." I didn't want him worrying, but I also didn't want him trying to stop me.

"Uh huh. And if I said anything to get you to back off, I suspect I would be in the doghouse." He lifted an eyebrow.

I shrugged a shoulder and gave a slight grin.

His eyes glanced away, "I suspect that is your informant at the door trying to get your attention." He pointed with his chin.

At the entrance to the restaurant was a pretty twenty-something girl in a maid's uniform with a purse over her shoulder. She waved when I looked her way and motioned to join her. I walked out as casually as possible, hoping to not draw attention. I led her to a tucked away corner of the hallway behind an impressive potted Bamboo Palm so we wouldn't be overheard.

"Audrey says I'm to report to you." Her chocolate eyes danced with excitement while her tone was matter of fact.

"Yes, I need you to gather what employees may hear from guests about the man who died last night.

Parts of conversations that may indicate who would want to hurt him or why. Then get with me and tell me what you find." I kept my voice low, just above a whisper.

She looked around before answering, "Can I just call you, like on your cell? We can set up a time. That way I can call if I'm alone in a room and nobody will know. Plus, I can't stop my work to track you down, you know." I liked how she was already working this into her workday, considering how to juggle the extra duties.

"Good point. Calling me will be fine." She took out her cell phone and entered my number..

"I don't imagine we'll get anything tonight and you're probably on your way home. How about nine tomorrow morning and then again at three in the afternoon if there is more to report?" I glanced around to check we weren't being watched. Nobody seemed to have noticed us.

"Okay. I'll call in the morning. Don't worry, we hear all kinds of stuff all the time. The guests think most of us don't speak English so they talk about anything around us." She smiled and then slipped away.

I returned to my table with Mason to find another round of drinks waiting for me. I sat and looked over the menu. Mason ordered the Bison Short Ribs, and I chose the Salmon filet, all very posh and healthy sounding with locally sourced vegetables. We were just relaxing when a woman walked up to the table. She wore a fire red clingy dress that left little to the imagination.

"Hi, Mason. Imagine running into you here." She was blond, thin, with perfect makeup and cleavage I would never have without implants. She was exactly what I imagined him dating, and nothing like me.

I looked at Mason with my eyebrows raised to my hairline.

Mason swallowed and looked between this interloper and me. "Tiffany, may I introduce you to my girlfriend, Julienne. Ma bichette, this is an *old* friend, Tiffany." He made a point of using his pet name for me in French, meaning little doe. She didn't even glance at me or acknowledge me in the teensiest way.

His ex girlfriend was named Tiffany, just like my high school nemesis back home. This didn't bode well.

He clenched his jaw and his eyes squinted. "I thought you didn't like the sun because it caused wrinkles? This isn't your sort of place."

"Oh, don't be that way, tiger. You've always been so passionate." Her eyes were locked onto him as if he were the only lifeboat on the Titanic and she would plow over anyone getting in her way.

Mason reached across, took my hand and kissed it while looking into my eyes. "Sorry Tiffany, we're having a romantic dinner. Goodbye." His eyes bore into mine with determination and purpose, like he was willing me to forget this incident while showing her he was all mine. His touch was a warm caress.

She placed a hand on his shoulder as she passed by, "Oh, you can count on it, tiger." The hostess sat *Tiffany* a few tables away with a menu. She stopped at our table on her way back and whispered, "You're from the new owner, right?" I nodded. "Want me to mess up her order or something?" She winked.

"No, but can you delay her meal so we can leave well before she finishes?."

"You got it, hun. I'll put a rush on yours as well."

Mason let out his breath and shook his head. "I'm sorry about that. Her behavior is inexcusable."

I tried to keep the jealousy that was percolating up tamped down. "You had to deal with my old boyfriend during our breakup when you were just my neighbor helping me out." I took a big swallow of my Margarita, "Plus, I know you were a Casanova before we got together. She confirms what I thought your tastes ran, though." In other words, not me.

"She is what I thought would make me happy. But, she is shallow, superficial, and self-serving. You are beautiful inside as well as out." His eyes never left my face. I smiled at the open flattery, I wasn't used to it.

"You're telling me that all the *tiger* references didn't

work to remind you of how *close* you two were and want that again?"

"No, it did *not* work. I remember all the terrible times. And just to set the record straight, I was never just your neighbor. I wouldn't interfere with a couple, but once you broke up, I wasn't about to lose any time in getting closer to you. I noticed you the day I was moving in and couldn't get you out of my system." His eyes were hungry for more than our dinner. I was feeling a bit warm and tingly all over from his gaze and wondering how long before we were alone in our room. Oh my!

As if on cue, our dinner arrived. Mason released my hand reluctantly so he could eat. It was all delicious, but we seemed in a hurry to finish and escape to the room. We must have finished in record time and scurried up to our room at breakneck speed.

I was nervous about taking our relationship to the next level, so I bought a sexy hot red negligee. I slipped into the bathroom to put it on, but I made the mistake of looking in the mirror and all my nerves returned. It took all my courage to open the door and step out, only to find Mason sound asleep. He was propped up like he was waiting for me. His bare chest and chiseled abs took my breath away. The long drive yesterday, being up late because of murder, and early morning plus traipsing around in the desert all day and a full stomach with alcohol in his tea must have been too much for him. I changed into my regular cotton PJs and joined him, partly disappointed and partly relieved. Especially when I thought about *Tiffany* and how perfect I bet she looked in a negligee.

CHAPTER 5

The next morning Mason was up well before dawn to take his sunrise photos in the first spot he picked. He gave me a tender kiss. "Today will be better, Ma bichette." Then the door softly closed.

I dressed in another of my standard skirt suits. I chose a peach colored blazer and matching skirt with a white blouse so it was more summery. But I wore flat shoes because I didn't know what the day would bring. When I made it to the offices to check in on each of the management team's progress with the homework from yesterday, Audrey waved me into her small space.

"Jonathan wants to wait until this afternoon. That will give us a little longer to get familiar on the practice site and do the homework you gave us." She paused and took a breath, "It'll also give you the morning to question any suspects you have in mind. I guess he's eager for you to make some progress." She studied my face, her mouth in a frown. Either she was frustrated at the delay in training or she was worried about me.

I wasn't happy about the change in plans, but what could I do when the owner, my boss's boss, was pushing Jonathan and thus me to investigate? The bad news was I didn't have a clue or a suspect for a starting point.

I shrugged a shoulder to appear casual about the change, "I can get with Graciella and find out if there is any gossip filtering in to point me to a suspect." I kept my voice low key so as not to encourage much hope in this route.

She smiled and relief washed over her face. The staff was probably anxious because the murder of a guest is a scary occurrence, but the timing of just being bought by a new owner was probably even more nerve racking..

I left the office area and debated what to do until Graciella called with the first report. My choices were to walk the grounds and get a better idea of the layout of the resort, go back to my room, or go to the Canyon Cafe and have some coffee and maybe a little something for breakfast. I opted for coffee first.

The early breakfast crowd was just trickling out and I got seated right away. I scanned the tables and didn't recognize the people present as part of Howell Venture.

They probably had a continental breakfast in their main conference room.

Sun was streaming in through the enormous picture windows along one wall. The nature sounds from the speakers enveloped me and the muscles in my shoulders relaxed. I needed this sound track for home.

At the entrance, I saw Blair in a lovely coordinated floral blouse and skirt and beaten up old canvas sneakers waiting to be seated. Her clothes seemed a smidge baggy, and I wondered once again if she had a health condition causing weight loss. I waved her over to join me. She waved back and threaded her way through the tables.

She sat down and heaved a sigh, "I slept in late today, normally I'm an early riser."

I smiled, "I'm not, really. Always have been a late sleeper which doesn't fit with most jobs."

We both studied our menus. Healthy options were plentiful with a few standard offerings plus the resort's added flare.

Blair leaned over to me, "I recommend their Cranberry Pecan French Toast. I've a sensitive stomach or I would get that myself."

I folded my menu, "That sounds amazing. You've sold me."

When the server came, I noticed Blair ordered the Granola and Yogurt Parfait, which was the cheapest item for breakfast. Not that there was anything wrong with that, but I wondered if there was more than her health going on in her life. Perhaps after her husband's passing, the finances weren't as plentiful as before. I'd heard of that happening many times.

"Yesterday you said you used to come here often with your husband. Were you aware of the bow and arrow on display in the library?" I might as well make this a working breakfast and see if there was anything Blair knew from past stays at Enchantment Canyon Resort.

"Oh my, yes. I remember hearing the tale about the vengeful brave from a local Native American man who did a program one evening here about the local folklore and legends. It was all so fascinating." She got that faraway look in her eyes as she remembered happier times, with her husband no doubt.

"I wonder if there is any way to speak to him. Do you remember his name, by any chance?" It was a long shot, but maybe it would help to know more about why Merritt Howell thought the curse killed him.

"Mmm, I don't. Maybe someone on staff still has him come out occasionally and can help you connect with him." She said before taking a sip of her herbal tea.

That was actually an excellent idea. I would follow up on that this afternoon.

"I wonder... Since you've been here before, had you stayed when the Howell Venture Capital Firm was doing a retreat?" I didn't want to appear like I was interrogating her, but I had to start somewhere.

"Yes, I believe so. But, I'm afraid I couldn't tell you anything about them. It was a few years back, and it's not like I got to know any of them personally to provide any insights." My initial hope at her affirmative reply died quickly.

Our food came, so the chatting stopped as we sank into our separate thoughts while eating. I was mentally reviewing what Audrey had told me the night of the murder. The first bit of gossip she overheard in a bar over drinks that Connor was aiming, no pun intended, to take over Merritt's job. Yesterday he seemed to step into the leadership role when greeting the executives in the morning, as though he had already assumed the mantle. How could I speak to him or find out more?

He sure seemed too friendly with Merritt's wife, Margaux, who had been hanging all over him rather than shedding tears at the crime scene. But to be fair, Merritt ignored her through dinner from what I saw and was too busy flirting with another woman. Still, that gave Margaux a motive. That made two people already on my list, and I hadn't begun yet. Could Connor and Margaux have killed him together, a joint effort? At least it was a starting point.

I hadn't seen the woman Merritt had texted during dinner that night. She didn't seem connected to the company or hanging with any of the corporate people. What if he was on his way to a rendezvous with her and a jealous boyfriend or husband ended their affair? It could be that simple, couldn't it?

A jealous husband made sense, except for the arrow. Somebody took the time to remove the bow and arrow from the case in the library. That was evidence of planning and deliberate actions, not a heated moment or accident.

Before I knew it, Blair had finished first and left the table, wishing me a pleasant rest of the day. I was too preoccupied to be good company. I launched out of my chair, determined to get as much done this morning as possible.

I began at the registration desk with Maria.

"Hi, Maria. A returning guest told me about a wonderful talk that a Native American gentleman gave a few years back. He shared local legends and such. Is there any way to get in contact with the man?" I smiled and tried to rein in my urgency to get something moving on my inquiries. The killer could check out and make it harder all around. Tick, tock.

"That would be Miguel RunningElk. He hasn't been here in a month or so. I think I have his contact information in a file. Just a moment." She stooped over and opened a two-drawer file cabinet. She thumbed through file folders and eventually removed one and glanced through the information. "I have a phone number, but that is all. I think it is a landline even." She wrote the number down for me.

I accepted the slip of paper and tapped it against my chin. Should I call right away? How should I proceed, and what should I say to him? I'd have to think a little about how to approach Mr. RunningElk.

A door down the hall opened and about thirty people wandered out, all talking on phones or texting. The Howell Venture Firm must be taking a break. Many immediately made their way to the restrooms, but several, including the widow Margaux, walked out to the smoking area outside. The designated area was a patio isolated from the rest of the resort. It comprised a large concrete area with many potted and hanging plants. A privacy fence enclosed the space. It was surprising to find a smoking area at a health and wellness resort, but I suppose you tackle one habit or issue at a time. Perhaps that's why it's so removed from the usual open flow, so those attempting to quit weren't tormented.

I glanced at my watch. It was a few minutes before Graciella was scheduled to call me, but who knew if she would call right at nine or wait until her maid duties made it easier to stop. I made my decision of what to do on a hunch.

I don't smoke, but I walked out to join the widow and get some gossip! The heat was like a wall you walked into. It took me only a few seconds to realize I should have tried to get cigarettes from an employee to make it look like I belonged here before walking out. I began patting my blazer and pant pockets as if I was suddenly missing my "smokes".

I glanced over at Margaux, "Can I bum a cig from you?" I crossed my fingers that I sounded like one of them.

Margaux looked me up and down and I became even more self-conscious than usual about my few extra pounds and business clothes where she looked like a fashion plate with her designer dress and Jimmy Choo heels.

Without saying a word, she dug a long slender cigarette and Cartier lighter out from her Chloé bracelet purse. She was adept at rubbing your face in her wealth without saying a word. What struck me more than anything was how refreshed she looked for a widow. Not a hint of grief strained her perfectly coiffed hair or made-up face.

I accepted the cigarette, placed it in my mouth, and leaned in for the light. I fought hard not to choke and cough at the stringent smoke in my mouth that I blew out immediately after I puffed on the cigarette. Between that and the heat, I was in danger of my breakfast coming up.

Another woman smoking on the patio laughed, "I think she's turning green," She stepped closer. "You okay there?"

Smiling, I tried to laugh it off, "It's been awhile. I quit but keep coming back." I am a better liar than my cousin, but that doesn't mean much at the moment. Fighting the urge to cough up a lung, I swallowed several times. My eyes teared up from the smoke. Then I realized my clothes were going to smell now. *What was I thinking?*

Margaux smiled, which was more of a wicked grin, "You've never smoked before in your life." She squints and assesses me again. "You're the little employee who found Merritt's body." It's a statement rather than a question and I can't deny it, but I won't confirm it either. The way she said "little employee" made me feel like an invisible servant. Most widows would vividly remember who found their husband dying. A shiver coursed up my spine to see such cold-blooded disregard.

I was about to snuff the cigarette and count this as a failure when she spoke again, "Trying to get some bit of juicy gossip to share with the other employees?" Her voice was saccharine sweet and that wicked grin was back.

I hadn't said a word, and perhaps that was working best. Looking her in the eye, I shrugged one shoulder. I tried for a curious look, as if I'd never been around the wealthy and privileged before in my life. At my full-time job at the Colorado Springs Resort, I dealt with international wealth every day and she didn't impress me.

My lack of sharing must bother her because she fills the silence, "I know what all of you are thinking." She inhales deep from her cigarette, "Look, my marriage wasn't the happiest. I don't expect *you* to understand." Her statement reeked of condescension.

My mouth took off on its own, "I know he ignored you for other women and treated you as stupid." I snapped my mouth shut and wished I could snatch back my words. I blamed it on the heat and cigarette causing a lack of oxygen to my brain.

I expected her to take offense, so it surprised me when her eyes lit up. "Yes, exactly. I spent years with that treatment. So, maybe I don't cry over his death. I feel like I've been released from a cruel tormentor." But did she have a part in her sudden freedom?

I raised an eyebrow.

She pursed her lips, "Oh, I didn't kill him. I'm too sensitive a soul to murder anybody. Besides, I was with

Connor." I nearly choked, keeping my harsh laugh stuffed down deep. She pointed her smoldering cigarette at me, "But, I'll tell you who had a good reason to kill him. That Preston Richards. Merritt added another notch on his bedpost with Preston's wife, hand to God." She nodded.

CHAPTER 6

*A*h ha! Another person to add to my list. Now I was getting somewhere. But Margaux retreated into silence.

I had to keep her talking, defending herself if I was going to get anything more. "Which one is Preston?" Not very inspired, but that's all I could think of that was just gossipy without slipping into interrogation mode and being obvious. The night Merritt was killed, Audrey pointed him out in the crowd of gawkers. Thin, forties, balding, and an exec of some sort was all I remembered.

"He's that scrawny, ugly guy. You'd think he could afford some hair treatment and a gym membership." She inhaled deep from her cigarette and squinted at me again. "He started working at the company the same time as Merritt. He was always Merritt's loyal lapdog, too. But Merritt just had to ruin the friendship with his inability to keep it in his pants. It would serve him right if that's what got him killed." Wisps of smoke escaped as she spoke.

She snapped her fingers and pointed the cigarette at me again, "I just remembered, they weren't so close recently. Merritt even said he wished Preston wasn't attending this year. Preston must've known about them and finally saw Merritt for his true snake-in-the-grass self."

My cigarette had died out from lack of attention. I rubbed it into a sand filled urn and turned to leave. "My breaks over." I muttered as I ducked back into the resort. What I really wanted to tell her was the resort had a smoking cessation program she should consider.

I took a deep breath of unadulterated air. I felt dirty from that exchange, and it wasn't from the smoke. Why did people stay together if they're miserable? Sure, she probably stayed for the money and status. Maybe she thought his humiliating her and being unfaithful was worth the clothes and money. But why would he stay if he didn't even like her? Staying with somebody just to have arm candy for your plus one made little sense to me. I shook my head.

I headed back to the lobby like a homing pigeon when my cell phone rang. Graciella.

"Hello, Julienne speaking." I sat in one of the rustic

chairs by the rounded fireplace in the lobby.

"It's Graciella. I have a little to report." She was efficient and to the point.

"Is there a lot, do I need to write this down?" I could get something at the reception desk.

"I don't think so. So far everyone is pointing fingers at each other. But this tidbit might be important. Seems the dead man had ruined his partner in the business. The old partner lost his family, friends, house everything because of it." She took a breath. It sounded as though she were pushing her housekeeping cart. I heard a guest ask for more towels. Eventually, she returned to our conversation, "The reason that's important is this man, the partner, he's in town and a guest said she saw him here. The rest is petty stuff about each other."

Wow, that was significant. "Thank you, Graciella. That helps. Any idea of the guy's name?"

"No, sorry ma'am. I will call later if I get more." She said just before hanging up. I guess we were done. It would have been nice to have the name, but I could probably find it online later.

The Howell Venture Capital executives were returning to their meeting. I watched on the other side of a Monstera plant. The meeting or who attended wasn't a secret, so I don't know why I did it. I leaned against the wall as if I were just casually relaxing and texting on my phone. Margaux entered last, and Connor looked up and down the hallway before closing the door to the large room.

Why was Margaux in the meeting if she were only a spouse? The other spouses weren't attending the meetings. Did she inherit stock or any say in the company now? Or perhaps Connor was trying to look good by having the support of Merritt's widow to help him assume control of the firm.

My phone rang again, this time with the ringtone, Moon River, indicating Beverly. I envisioned my spunky elderly neighbor as I answered. Maybe I could fill in a few more pieces to this puzzle with her help.

"Good morning, Beverly." I walked outside while talking to her. From the lobby I went out the back door to the courtyard, outdoor pool, and the path to the landscaped park-like garden with the crime scene tape. Even in the shade of a flowering tree, I could feel sweat on my forehead and the back of my neck.

"Hello dear. Is it sizzling there? I hear its elevation keeps it from being too hot, but the weather channel is reporting record highs." Beverly wasn't obsessed with weather, but probably came close. I took the long way around the pool to avoid the noise and found a more private section to talk under another leafy tree.

"It feels rather hot, sure." I tried to avoid dwelling on it. I didn't want the usual "but it's a dry heat" discussion. "So, did you find anything on Merritt Howell?"

"Of course, ye of little faith," She scoffed. "Whittaker Tate, who started the company, was the CEO and Merritt was Chief Operating Officer until a surprising removal from office six years ago when Merritt took over and removed Tate and his name."

"That sounds like there is more to the story." I said as I ducked further into the shade of the landscaped garden area, seeking cooler air.

"You know it. It seems there was a lot of speculation at the time why Tate was pushed out. The company lost a lot of credibility and many suspected Merritt of an internal struggle to take over." She became quiet.

"What are you holding back?" She usually would provide her own commentary.

"Whittaker Tate lost everything. He went bankrupt, lost his house and friends, his wife even committed suicide. I don't want you going after him. He's suffered enough." This coincided with what Graciella had supplied about the prior partner's sad fate. Beverly's compassion towards a suspect surprised me. Perhaps because she had lost her husband, albeit not to suicide but kidney disease.

"We don't know how he lost the company. But if he blamed Merritt Howell for everything that happened to him, he would have plenty of motive to kill Merritt." If Merritt had something to do with Mr. Tate losing everything, then perhaps he would think it was the curse getting him back.

I recalled the words on the display rack for the bow and arrow in the library. *"vengeance is about to be delivered to an evil man"* and then *"...as a symbol to all who have done evil that their reward will be swift like an arrow to the heart."* It seemed to me somebody took the vengeance aspect of the story as inspiration when they plunged an arrow into Merritt's heart. Mr. Tate sounded like a viable suspect. I paced under a set of trees.

"Do you know where this Whittaker Tate lives?" I plowed ahead despite Delores' reluctance.

"No, I don't. But the chances of him being anywhere near there have got to be slim." She said. Not if the information Graciella reported was accurate, and he was seen at the resort.

"Okay. Can you research the rest of the executives for me, as well? I have to look into this for the owner, Mr. Carlton, and I would like as much factual information on the executives of the company as possible." I would have to look up more on Tate myself, apparently.

"I'm on it." She hung up and I could feel her anger. She knew I wasn't going to forget Whittaker Tate in my suspicions. This wasn't the first time one of my helpful neighbors wasn't pleased with my questions or suspect list during an investigation. Tate had such a robust motive I had to consider him. If he lost everything, he would have to kill Merritt himself rather than hire somebody. Graciella's information indicated a guest saw Tate here.

I made my way to the reception desk and ever helpful Maria. "Can you do me a favor and see if Whitaker Tate is staying here?" She tapped away on her computer terminal. "No, the last time he was a guest here was two years ago." Her phone rang, so I thanked her and walked to the guest lounge area and sat. I took out my cell phone and took notes of everything so far.

Who was Merritt texting with? Could that woman have lured him into the garden? Could her husband, if she had one, have killed Merritt?

Connor was a suspect as he was too friendly with Merritt's wife and wanted to take over the company as head honcho. Hopefully Delores would supply his last name and what he did at the company.

Then there was Margaux, the merry widow who alibied Connor, and thus herself. Who also appeared to not shed a single tear over her husband's murder and said it was like being freed from a tormentor. I wanted to know if she inherited Merritt's money or any interest or shares in the company. I doubted I could easily uncover the details of Merritt's will.

Preston, who Margaux claimed had a falling out with Merritt because he got sleazy with Preston's wife, was another person of interest. I needed to find out if that's true or not.

Finally Whittaker Tate, the former CEO who reportedly lost everything when he was removed from the company. Did he blame Merritt for his tragic luck and the suicide of his wife? Was he really here at the resort, perhaps under an alias, or was that someone's imagination, or a convenient diversion?

That was a lot for just beginning. There were already plenty of people who seemed to have a motive to kill him. This was going to take some time to dig into, and I still had more training to conduct.

I glanced at my watch; I had a little over an hour before lunch and then the afternoon sessions with the management team. It would be nice if I could talk to at least one more of the people on my list. I got up and went to the reception desk one more time. I had to wait a few minutes as she checked out a couple.

"Maria, can I ask you a question about the Howell Venture Firm?" I kept my voice low just in case guests wandered past.

"Absolutely."

"Do you know what their schedule is? Do they have time that they join in activities?"

She turned her back on the lobby and lowered her

voice, "Are you wanting to talk to some of them away from the rest of the pack sort of thing?"

I nodded.

"Well, they don't let out until three usually. They even have lunch together in their meeting rooms." She glanced around and made sure nobody was in the lobby, "I'd go crazy being stuck with them that long every day."

I chuckled. It looked like I couldn't do anything more until after my training time. Except...

"Maria, how could I find a person if they are staying in town? This person was seen around here, but he isn't staying here."

"I can give you a list of the other upscale hotels in town and you can call them." She wrote five hotel names on a slip of paper for me, and I tucked them in my blazer pocket. I was standing with Maria when the entrance door opened and in walked Tiffany in her blond brilliance. She wore designer dress and heeled shoes. I had at least thirty pounds more than her, and I never aspired to be a model like she seemed to be emulating. She did the runway prance to the registration desk.

"I need the room number for Mason Sheridan, please." Maria tapped a few keys, then looked at me.

I took over rather than Maria being stuck in the middle, "Our guest's privacy is a top priority and we can't give out room numbers. Can I help you with anything? If you leave him a message, I'll make sure he gets it." Oh boy, would I.

She looked me up and down. "You're his little fling girl, aren't you?" She leaned in over the registration top, "Honey, you're in over your head. He's slumming for a little while with you, nothing more. I can't imagine what he sees in you, anyway." She turned and pranced to the elevator, her high heels clacking on the tile floor.

Maria and I looked at each other, I raised an eyebrow. "She needs a dose of reality."

I didn't want to be ugly, but the woman had shaken me. *His little fling and slumming!*

"At least I'm not trying to be a model in the middle of a desert in a heat wave." slipped out. I didn't even realize the thought had entered my head before it was out for the world to hear. I slapped my hand over my mouth.

Maria giggled and nodded.

But I had to wonder why she was trying to call Mason. I had a bad feeling about this. I tamped down my concerns and focused on my next few hours.

I sat in the lobby again and called the hotels Maria had given me. I started with the big hotel and casino off Highway 285 on Buffalo Trail. It was very popular, but it was apparently not Mr. Tate's style. On the third hotel I found Mr. Whittaker Tate, former CEO before Merritt at a historical hotel on the plaza. Now I knew where he was staying, but bumping into him would be more difficult. Perhaps Mason and I could do dinner at Tate's hotel on the plaza and try to *bump* into him.

I was contemplating this when a resort employee, Emilio by his name tag, handed me a note. "Sorry to interrupt, but this was left outside your room on the carpet." He handed me a small envelope. Emilio scurried away, and I opened the envelope with care. I didn't know what to expect. If it was staff, they could find me or leave a message with Maria or Audrey. I didn't know any of the other guests enough for them to know my room number.

In block print was handwritten: *I have information, meet in the sauna at 11.* I looked around, but nobody was lurking and watching me. I found it interesting somebody left the note outside my room. That revealed my specific room was common knowledge, and I didn't feel comfortable with that. It also took a risk that I wouldn't get the note in time for the meeting. Unless they knew an employee would get it to me. Hmmm.

It was only a few minutes before eleven and the meet time. I didn't like that somebody singled me out when nobody should know I was more than curious in Merritt's murder other than the staff. Maybe it was an employee who didn't want to give their information through Graciella, but talk to me directly. That would explain why the note was left at my room, especially if they knew I wasn't training until this afternoon. *Sure, that was it. Just an employee. Nothing to worry about.*

I walked over to Maria and got directions to the sauna and let her know I was meeting somebody there. If I didn't return or call her in twenty minutes, she was to send somebody looking for me. I like to believe I'm not completely reckless.

I walked down quiet halls and passed the indoor pool with a water aerobics class in session and the half full exercise room. I entered the women's locker room and walked through it to the joint sauna.

The steam was thick, but I seemed to be alone as I stood in the doorway. I didn't really want to go into all the dripping steamy heat with my work clothes and my cell phone, but I didn't have time to change. Oh well, it couldn't be helped. I stepped inside and stood to one side. I didn't want to sit on the wet wooden bleachers in my work clothes either. The soft lighting and steam made it seem dreamlike. I glanced at my watch, a minute after eleven. Occasionally I could hear a muffled voice in one of the locker rooms nearby. I paced. Five minutes after. The heat seemed stifling in all my clothes. Five minutes later and my clothes were damp and my hair was limp. I wasn't waiting any longer and turned to leave, but the door wouldn't open.

I felt around for a lock of any sort. Nothing. My hands ran over the door, but I didn't find any special trick to opening it. I wasn't worried, I could always turn off the steam and heater in the corner, right? Hoping somebody in one of the locker rooms would hear me, I banged on the door. I stopped and listened, but there wasn't any sound outside. I pounded on the door again and finally heard voices. My fists beat on the door harder until it finally opened.

A rush of cool, dry air washed over me. Blair was looking at me with a long cylinder of some sort in her hand.

"Thanks for opening the door." I managed.

"Somebody lodged this against the door so you couldn't open it." She held it up.

I looked at it closer. The metal cylinder had rubber on one end so it wouldn't slide on the floor, and the top had a V shape to fit against a doorknob or handle. I had seen these for people who fear intruders in hotel rooms.

"Thanks again. Did you see anybody leaving the area?" It was a long shot, but I gave it a try.

"No, nobody was around. I just stopped to use the bathroom after my water aerobics and heard you banging," she said. I noticed she was in a bathing suit with a towel around her.

"Well, no harm," I tossed out attempting to make light of the situation.

"I think you need to change out of those clothes, they are drenched." She observed.

"I'm going to go do that now." I left in a hurry.

It was evident somebody knew I was asking questions and didn't like it. In my room, I made it to a chair before my nerves got the better of me and my legs began shaking. The stunt wasn't meant to harm me, just scare me. Okay, it worked. I was shaken.

But the staff were the only people who knew I was tasked with looking into the murder for the resort. Either a staff member didn't like my intrusion or they had blabbed to others. Both were feasible, and my quietly asking around without notice was no longer possible. I would keep gently asking questions, but I would rely on gossip again.

I changed and dried my hair; I had just enough time to grab lunch and get back to training the management team. I left a note for Mason that I would like to have dinner on the plaza in downtown Santa Fe if he was up to it and why.

I was on auto-pilot during training. Thank goodness I knew the software inside and out and didn't have to think. I barely finished with Jonathan when Graciella called again. I ducked into a supply closet to talk.

"Graciella, got anything for me?" I looked at the

floor polisher and various equipment.

"The company-retreat people are mostly talking about who is going to take over. It looks like Preston somebody, and Connor are the most likely. Other talk is what the widow is going to do now. Some think she will try to latch onto Connor even though he's married, while others think Connor will dump her if he takes control of the company. They don't seem to even care who may have killed Mr. Howell." She said with naked disgust.

That wasn't helping my plan to rely on gossip if they weren't gossiping about the murder. There was still my earlier scare in the Sauna.

"Do the company people know I'm looking into the murder for the resort?"

Graciella let out a sigh, "I don't know how it happened, but yes. They know and ask each other if you have talked to them. I'm sorry. I didn't tell them, I promise." Anxiety in her voice spoke louder than her words.

"Don't worry, I'm not mad. It's hard to keep some things a secret. Just keep listening, okay?" It could have been an employee or one of my suspects who trapped me in the sauna, hard to say without a witness. I still didn't think it was intended to hurt me, but that didn't mean I wasn't taking it seriously.

I hung up from Graciella and saw a text message

from Mason pop up saying he was making reservations to the upscale restaurant at the Tate's hotel in town on the Plaza. The Plaza, I found out from the hotel website, was the original city square with a park in the center and historic buildings surrounding it on four sides. It had cafes, art galleries, various gift stores all along the four sides. One side of the plaza was a long-standing 5-star hotel with its own restaurants. Often there were folks selling native bead-work jewelry and goods on the Plaza sidewalks. I was glad to see a little of the town while I was here.

I took my job in resort management because it was my opportunity to see the world. I had dreams of managing resorts around the world. That had been a deal breaker with my last boyfriend, Brandon, who wanted to settle down and maybe take a vacation once in a while with a horde of children. I wanted to travel as part of my work, and I had no desire to have children at all.

My father fought me often on both points as he wanted me to be a country club wife giving him grandchildren to spoil. My mother died of breast cancer when I was twelve, so I didn't have her to run interference and talk to dad. Mason agreed with me on both counts. He loved traveling and could do photography from anywhere, and he was in no hurry to have children, if ever. Another reason I was amazed we were together after thinking I was such a rarity I'd never find a life-partner.

In my room, I got ready for dinner while Mason showered the desert away. Somehow we still hadn't taken the step into physical intimacy, even though we fell asleep in each other's arms. He was dressing in the bathroom and I took the time to check my email.

I was hoping Beverly had emailed me with some research. Sure enough, she had sent me some preliminary information. Thankfully, she had included a brief article about Whittaker Tate that had a photo of the man, so I knew who I was looking for tonight. I took a picture of the photo on my laptop with my cell phone, so I had it handy for reference.

When Mason stepped out of the bathroom, he had dressed. He wore soft tan slacks that were tailored to fit, a button down crisp shirt in cobalt blue, and leather loafers. He definitely had style and knew what looked good on him.

I HAD CHANGED into a summer dress of red with white swiss dots that was knee-length with a sweetheart neckline and slim skirt. I wore comfortable pump shoes to match. Thanks to my cousin Felicia's fashion sense and determination to show me to my best advantage, I brought this dress plus a few other items. I wasn't an hourglass figure; I wasn't curvy but more straight lines, but the dress made it look like I had curves. My hair was pulled back and a few curled strands left to frame my face, just as Felicia had trained me to do.

Mason stopped when he saw me and gulped. He let out a whistle.

"You take my breath away." He said with an appreciative look.

I blushed, I wasn't used to such praise. I waved my hand in a "oh, stop it" motion, but kept from kicking a shoe on the carpet in my embarrassment.

"You clean up well yourself." I managed to reply.

He took me in his arms with a chuckle at my shyness. "Is this dinner part of your investigating the murder or just a need to experience this restaurant?"

I pulled away and found him grinning at me. He really got me. It felt good.

I laughed, "A little of both. The food sounds amazing, and the hotel is such a historic icon of Santa Fe I want to see it. The bonus is a suspect is staying there that we might run into."

I shared my information on Whittaker Tate with him, including the photo.

"I'm ready to play your wingman with him. I'm just glad I'll be there with you." He said as he chucked my chin. I sure wasn't telling him about being locked in the Sauna now!

CHAPTER 7

*T*he hotel took an entire block on one side of the Plaza and was a classic Spanish Colonial adobe style with a soft buttery tan color that glowed. Inside were red tile floors and the same tan walls with occasional terracotta red accents. The ceiling was criss-crossed with dark timber planks supporting off-white decorative panels. The lobby's conversation seating area was rustic with leather and wood furnishings and Native American art mixed with local Hispanic art. We asked directions to the restaurant and made our way past multitudes of impressive art and displays representing Santa Fe history.

The restaurant was an indoor oasis, inviting and magical. The outer walls consisted of frosted floor-to-ceiling paned glass panels with hand painted Spanish folk art on the glass. Natural light poured in from large skylights and an impressive black wrought iron chandelier with amber glass hurricane globes hung over a softly splashing romantic fountain. Trees in large planters were interspersed among the tables with white twinkle lights woven through the branches. The tables were glossy dark wood with matching carved wood high-back chairs. The atmosphere was of rustic elegance and magical.

I realized this was our first romantic date in the months we had been together. Mason held my chair for me and after scooting me up to the table, he leaned over and whispered, "All eyes are on you, mon chéri."

I blushed again and gulped. My heart was racing.

We started with a bottle of Spanish Tempranillo wine and the signature Tortilla Chicken soup and the Roasted Green Chile and Corn Chowder. We shared the soups since they were both delicious. For the main course Mason ordered the char-grilled steak enchilada with red and green sauce and I had a southwestern pasta dish with roasted butternut squash, caramelized onions, spiced walnuts, and a fire roasted tomato cream sauce. We gave each other tastes but stuck to our choices.

I was relaxing and smiling like a fool. It was romantic, and I felt like a princess with my prince. Too soon, dinner was over. I wished it would never end, but it was time to find Mr. Whittaker Tate.

We went to the check-in desk. I hadn't thought about how I would approach our search. Before I could fret or stumble for how to find our suspect, Mason took the lead.

"Hi there. We were to meet Whittaker Tate for drinks after our dinner to discuss some business, but I don't see him. Do you know if he's in the hotel tonight or if we missed him?" He smiled at the young lady behind the desk.

She smiled wide and fluttered her eyes at him and ignored me. Mason definitely had a way with people, particularly the ladies. "Mr. Tate, oh yes. I believe he is up at the rooftop bar. Take that elevator up." She pointed down a hall.

The rooftop bar appeared large enough for a capacity of eighty people standing, but tonight it had four sections with patio furniture full and the high bar tables about half full with a handful of people standing around in groups. All along the roof edge barrier was a long narrow table top and bar stools that could seat twenty-five or more and was two-thirds full of people watching the colorful sunset over a panorama of downtown Santa Fe and the historic buildings. It was like an artist had splashed glowing paint to bathe the buildings in splendor. We enjoyed the view at the edge for a few moments, then turned to survey the crowd for Whittaker Tate.

The fifty-something gentleman sat at a high round table by himself. His light blue button-down shirtsleeves were rolled up a few inches. He was nursing an amber liquid, perhaps whiskey or scotch, with ice. We stood next to his table until he looked up. He had thinning blond hair, an average face, but eyes that really looked at you and saw you.

"Can I help you?" His voice was direct, as if he was used to being heard without raising it. For a middle-aged man he looked like he was athletic and showed only a slight thickening at the middle.

Mason put his hand out, "I'm Mason and this is Julienne, we were hoping to talk to you. It'll only take a few moments of your time." He flashed his dazzling smile.

Whittaker Tate looked us up and down, "You don't appear to be reporters." He motioned his hand to take a seat.

I jumped right in, "Sir, I work at the resort and am trying to help get closure on Howell's death for them." I took a breath as he watched me. "Someone on staff saw you talking with Mr. Howell the day before his demise. I understand there might be bad blood between you, but I know you can also give me a good rundown of the others in Mr. Howell's orbit and their... motives." I surprised myself at my transparency. This was a man who would see right through any excuse I made to talk to him, so I went with honesty.

He leaned back and crossed his arms. His keen eyes seemed to take in everything, and I felt vulnerable. He leaned forward and placed his arms on the table.

"Okay, I'll share some insights. But first, I know you're thinking that I had the biggest motive of all with how he made my life hell in his campaign to push me out and take over. It took me a while to dig out of the pit of depression and self pity. But, I have put him and the whole ugly past behind me because it was tearing me apart. I got counseling and worked through the grief of my wife's suicide and I started over." He took a sip of his drink.

"I was at your resort. But I went to forgive him for what he did. It's part of my recovery. Probably the hardest words I've ever said, but I had to say it. For my sake, not his. He didn't even react, just turned around and walked away."

I glanced at Mason and we raised our eyebrows. I didn't know if I could forgive the man who tore my life to shreds.

I cleared my throat, "What about anybody else who might not be so enlightened?"

"Off the top of my head, Margaux would be a suspect. The prenuptial agreement would ensure she got zero, zip, if they divorced. And it wasn't like Merritt was a candidate for an early heart attack or anything. He was still in great health. I can see her deciding not to wait for her reward of putting up with his philandering and belittling." He mashed his lips together in thought.

"I also would place Yates Aldrich at the top of my list."

"I don't know who this Yates person is. You're the first to mention him." I prompted him.

"Yates is just like Merritt, just as cutthroat and dirty. He's also Merritt's biggest competitor in the business and a personal rival. They hate each other, probably because they are mirror images of each other in character. Plus the little known fact that Merritt slept with Yates' wife, Calista, to get insider information on Yates. Believe you-me, Yates would love to get even with Merritt in the worst way possible."

That was a significant new lead. "How would I get in touch with this Yates Aldrich? Is he even in town to begin with?" I don't want to waste time if the guy isn't even in the state.

"Oh, he's staying out at the casino hotel. I ran into him at the blackjack table last night." He eyed me again, "If you put on something slinky and low cut, he'll probably find you, since he hasn't had you yet." He gestured toward Mason with his glass, "That is if you can stand by long enough for her to get some info out of him. Sad to say, but the lady has the best chance of even speaking to him. He's that much of a dog." He stood up, tossed a few dollars on the table. "Best of luck folks, this interview is over."

He walked confidently away as we watched. It was a whirlwind of information.

Mason broke our silence, "Nothing new about the widow, but this Aldrich guy sounds repulsive." He looked me in the eye, "Please tell me you won't go near the lech without me there to back you up!"

"I guess we are dining at the casino tomorrow night. But I draw the line at wearing anything slinky for anybody but you." I cupped his face with my hand.

It was time to go back to the resort and call it a night. Twenty minutes later we were walking across the lobby of Enchantment Canyon Resort. I heard the clickity clack of high heels approaching fast behind me and my stomach flipped. I hadn't told Mason that Tiffany was determined to get time with him.

"Mason, darling." rang out through the lobby.

Mason let out a feral growl. With his skills in the military and as a bodyguard, I guessed that wasn't a good sign. He slipped his arm around my waist and spun me around with him. I put my arm around him as well and glared at *her*.

Tiffany was in a sexy, bright red gown more suited for the Oscars than a desert health and wellness spa, or for Yates Aldrich. Her lipstick and nail polish matched her dress. "I don't imagine she told you I was looking for you earlier? Let's have a cocktail, Tiger. We need to talk. I'm sure she can find her way by herself."

"I don't want to be cruel, Tiffany, but you have to stop. There is nothing between us. Nothing, no spark, no ember, nothing. I don't want to spend even this long with you. You are rude and intruding on my time with the woman I want to be with. That's not you, if you haven't gotten that clear yet." He spun us back around and we walked arm-in-arm to the elevator. As the elevator doors opened, she called out, "It's important, Mason."

Once we were in our room, his frustration vented.

"I can't believe her. I'm so sorry this has happened."

"What you said meant everything though, that I'm the one you want to be with." I put my arms around him and he gathered me into his arms and squeezed.

"I meant it." He let out a sigh, "She ruined the mood and we aren't getting it back tonight, are we?"

"It would be forced." I pulled back, tucked a wave of his hair back and smiled. "So long as we don't give up on us, we'll be fine." I said.

"I want us to enjoy our time together without pressure or stress."

I didn't sleep soundly. I woke up several times and

went over the suspects and motives. They swirled in my sleepy mind until the names melded together. Eventually I fell into a dream filled sleep. By morning, I was dragging and sluggish.

I walked through the lobby and noticed a security person still stationed at the front entrance, turning away reporters and camera crews.

I checked in with Audrey and the others on the management team, answered several questions on the software and made sure they were getting used to it. I would check their homework later. After only an hour, I was ready to start with three front desk agents to go over all the intricacies of the guest services job in the software. They would be the key staff to train the rest. This allowed me to spend quality time training a small number since we didn't have a training room with individual terminals for practice.

I was about to join the front desk folks when Graciella phoned.

I had barely answered when her words tumbled out, "You have to come quick, I don't know what to do with what I've found." She whispered. "Room 216, hurry." She hung up.

I stared at my cell phone for a few moments. I needed to back her up, so I shouldn't take time to think. What if a suspect caught her looking in their room ?

I turned to the front desk customer relations people

waiting for training, "I'll be back in about ten minutes and we can begin."

I sprinted to the elevator. I swear elevators can sense when I'm in a hurry and inch along, but when I need a moment to adjust my bra, they zoom up or down and the doors fly open. The elevator finally opened, and I zipped down the hall and screeched to a stop at 216 next to the housekeeping cart. The door flew open, Graciella must've been looking through the door peephole. She grabbed my arm and dragged me inside.

This was a spacious one-bedroom suite with a view of the landscaped garden and walking path from the balcony. It occurred to me that a person on the balcony could watch Merritt in the garden and guide the killer via cell phone directly to him with stealth.

Graciella was pale and wide eyed with a hand to her mouth and her other hand pointing to the bed. I looked at the half made bed and looked back at her.

"Look under the mattress on this side." She said.

I moved closer and could tell there was a tip or edge of something peeking out. I lifted the mattress and there was a Native American bow, probably the missing mate to the arrow that killed Merritt Howell. It certainly looked old and like it should be under glass safe from somebody sitting on it.

"I didn't know what to do. I was so shocked." Graciella said.

"Did you clean this room yesterday?"

She nodded yes.

"Was it there yesterday?"

She shook her head no.

"Whose room is this?" I braced myself for the answer.

"That arrogant Connor guy." She whispered.

Hmm. Suddenly the matching bow to the murder weapon shows up when it wasn't here before? I couldn't help but think the killer planted this evidence. Either the killer wanted to set up Connor to take the fall, or the killer really didn't want Connor to take over Howell Venture Capital. Or both.

"I'll call the detective on this case and go meet him in the lobby to bring him up. You lock the door and call security to stand outside, ok. Don't touch anything else, don't clean anything. Okay?"

She nodded. At least some color was coming back to her face. For a while, I thought she might pass out.

I exited the elevator on the ground floor and Carlos from security stepped in while I got out. I told him I was taking care of calling detective if he could secure the room.

Detective Sullivan answered on the third ring and said he would do our resort the courtesy of using an unmarked car and no siren. I thanked him heartily, but I suspected his reasons were more to avoid alerting the killer than any favor.

I then called Audrey to let her know what was happening, although Carlos had informed already them. Training was yet again on hold.

Fifteen minutes later Detective Sullivan jogged into the lobby with a backpack and we silently walked to the elevator together.

Once inside and the doors closed, he began his questions. No, I didn't find it. No, we didn't touch it. Yes, Carlos had secured the room.

Carlos stood outside the room with Graciella as she wrung her hands. Carlos opened the door and Graciella pointed again. Detective Sullivan put gloves on and took a large evidence bag from the backpack. He placed the bow in the evidence bag with care.

"Carlos, keep somebody posted here until the crime scene unit gets arrives. They're busy at a shooting and will be here in about thirty to forty-five. Nobody in or out." Then he turned to me, "I need someplace to talk to you two and the occupant of the room. Who would that be?" His eyes were hard and unforgiving.

"Connor, I don't know the last name. He's part of Howell Venture Capital." I shared

"We can use an empty room which might keep this from spreading to the guests." I couldn't help but protect the resort's reputation. He nodded and Graciella opened a room a few doors down the hall. He set the arrow and his backpack down on the bed.

He turned to me, "I want you to go get this Connor fella from his fancy company enclave meeting and bring him to me." It wasn't a request. I would hate to be a criminal in interrogation with this man. He now radiated an intensity that made it clear who was in charge.

When I started to say something he held up his hand, "I don't care how you get him here, just find an excuse to get him to go with you quietly." *Okay, now what LaMere?*

Oh, boy! What fun. How was I going to do that? I fretted over what to say to Connor all the way down in the elevator. I decided it was best to get him out of the meeting first, then deal with getting him upstairs to meet with Detective Sullivan.

I asked one of the customer relations agents at the front desk to slip into the meeting. Audrey had informed them I was pulled from training to work with the Detective and to assist. Maria slipped quietly into the meeting and reappeared with Connor a few moments later.

"What sort of emergency message?" He asked as he followed Maria to the front desk.

I stepped forward, "We're sorry to bother you sir,

but there is an emergency in your room." I figured if I got him up to his floor then the detective and Carlos could deal with any resistance from there.

His eyebrows bunched together in confusion, "What emergency in my room? Where is my wife? She should handle it, I'm busy."

"Your wife isn't available, so you must handle the situation. Please follow me." I began walking as though it was a command that he didn't dare disobey. It amazed me he followed.

Connor filled the ride up one floor with his grousing about being inconvenienced, and this would go on his review of his experience. I really wanted to lash out at one point and tell him he could have had a homicide detective drag his derriere out of the meeting in front of everyone, but I kept my mouth shut. Some people didn't know when they were being handed a favor. I knew the detective was now being generous to the resort by keeping a low profile, but that benefitted Connor and his jockeying for leadership of the company.

I texted the Detective to meet us at the elevator, so when the doors opened Detective Sullivan was waiting.

"Sir, I need to ask you a few questions. This way." He motioned with his hand to the left.

"What's this about? What's going on? Why is he here?" He glared at me as if I had purposely deceived him and was a conman. *Some people.* I didn't say a word, but I moved to where I could put a foot on his backside and shove him out of the elevator if needed. I would say I somehow tripped and knocked into him or something. Detective Sullivan smirked, either at Connor to show this was friendly or at my move to eject him.

"This way, please. Just a few questions."

I got my foot ready, but Connor stepped out of the elevator and followed the Detective. Whew! I really didn't want to test how he would have reacted if I shoved him into the Detective.

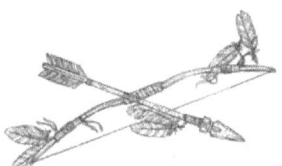

CHAPTER 8

I followed Detective Sullivan and fully expected him to bar me from the questioning, but he didn't even raise an eyebrow when I joined them. Could it be a courtesy to the resort so I could report to the management team? That was the only plausible explanation.

Inside the vacant room, Connor was fidgeting in a chair at the table next to the balcony. The suite was nicer than my basic accommodation. This room had jade green adobe walls, golden trim and accents, and turquoise green predominate in the fabric design used for the curtains and bedspread. The decor included local southwest artists for paintings. The bedroom had double doors separating it from the living area. It was posh, colorful, and had an updated Spanish feel. This had to be the nicest interrogation setting in history, but

I doubted Connor considered his good fortune. I stood back in a corner, just observing, don't mind me.

Connor began with bluster, "Look, I don't have time for this. You dragged me out of an important meeting --"

Detective Sullivan picked up the evidence bag, "Care to explain why I found this in your room?"

"What is…?" He gulped several times, making his Adam's apple bob up and down. "I don't know anything about that. It couldn't have been in my room. It just couldn't have been." He crossed his arms over his chest as if he refused to even hear it. But his bravado was shattered.

Detective Sullivan leaned close to Connor's face, "You are Connor Gallard and you are staying in room 216?"

"Yyy...eee...sss," he stuttered, then cleared his throat. "But that definitely wasn't in my room when I left this morning. And my wife sure as blazes doesn't have anything to do with it." His eyes were wide and dilated.

I believed him. Graciella would have found it under the mattress yesterday if it was there. But the police had given no indication of having any suspects, so the good detective would jump on this like my cousin on a half off shoe sale.

Detective Sullivan changed tactics, "Were you

sleeping with Merritt's wife as part of your campaign to step into Merritt's job? 'Cause I hear you would do *anything* to get that job and it's pay scale." Sullivan stayed in his face, watching every micro-expression flash across his face.

I saw shock and horror flash across his features, "It may sound suspicious, yes I was with Margaux when Merritt got killed. But there was nothing going on, I swear it." He was a terrible liar. His eye was twitching like a small electric shock hit it.

I let out an actual snort even though I meant to stay quiet.

Connor glanced at me and then back to the detective. His Adam's apple was bobbing again. "Margaux was just trying to make Merritt jealous and pay attention to her again. It was part of my mind games with Merritt, nothing more. But I never cheated on my wife."

I must have chuckled or something because he looked at me again, "What's so funny about that?"

Detective Sullivan turned to me with an eyebrow raised and motioned for me to speak.

"When I was checking in a few days ago you were at the elevator loudly proclaiming that these executive retreats weren't for any actual business, just wife swapping." I crossed my arms across my chest and tilted my head, as if to call his bluff.

Connor was pale and breathing shallow and quick. "I didn't mean anything by that." But his voice wasn't as assured, and I detected a note of pleading.

I may have thought that he was telling the truth about not bringing the bow to his room, but that didn't mean he didn't use it. In either case, his behavior was deplorable. It served him right to sweat a little over his predicament.

A shadow must have passed over the sun because the room took on a garish dark feel, like the joy in the brightly colored decor had been sucked out.

Detective Sullivan's voice picked up an *I'm done messing around* edge, "Enough of your covering for your reputation, this is murder I'm questioning you about not some fraternity pranks and male competition for girls. There is no statute of limitations for murder, and being a suspect for murder is a far worse blemish on your resume. It will follow you no matter where you go because I'll be sure every company you even consider knows I think you killed a man even if I can't prove it. Now get serious." I swallowed and felt nervous myself, but I think Connor stopped breathing.

"Yeah, sure. I get it. I'm serious when I tell you I don't know where that bow came from. Really, it wasn't me or my wife." He took a breath, licked his lips.

I noticed, and I'm sure the detective did as well,

that Connor was only proclaiming his innocence over the bow, not the murder.

"But I think you need to question Whittaker Tate about the argument I saw him having with Merritt the day before he was killed." He looked between the Detective and myself, seeking a sign we wouldn't hang him.

Detective Sullivan leaned back and smirked, "You're sure this was an argument, not just a lively discussion?"

I was surprised he appeared to know about Whittaker Tate. I guess he talked to Tate, or at least looked into him, already.

"Oh, it was an argument with their voices raised. Whittaker kept poking Merritt in the chest with his finger and yelling about killing his beloved wife." Connor's voice got stronger the more he was pointing the blame away from himself.

It wouldn't surprise me if Whittaker lied and did blame Merritt for his wife's suicide. He may have been telling the truth about trying to put it behind him because it was tearing him up, but then found out Merritt was at the resort. Maybe Tate even fought with himself over giving into the emotions he thought he had packed away and was finished with, only to drive out and confront the man who had taken everything precious from him. He may have gotten carried away, and the anger rushed out. But was it a cathartic release, or was it the beginning of rage that led to murdering Merritt in a premeditated action? I felt terrible for what he had been through, but if it pushed him to such violence, then he still had to face the consequences for his actions.

Detective Sullivan asked him several more pointed questions, but my mind was already churning through the bow's surprising appearance in Connor's room. If I didn't believe Connor placed the bow in his room, was somebody else trying to implicate him? Somebody who hated Merritt enough to kill him and hated Connor enough to hope he was arrested for the murder? That might be a long list considering what I was finding out about both men's character and low morals.

The cloud must have passed from the sun, because the room brightened and the colors exuded joy once again.

Detective Sullivan told Connor he could return to his meeting. Connor practically ran out the door. Detective Sullivan turned to me, "I know you met with Whittaker Tate last night. I had questioned him already. Did he tell you anything that may shed any light on this?"

Wow, color me shocked. At home, the police detective I had dealt with wasn't so calm about involving me. I shared what we talked about and my theory that he could have just had a cathartic release or the argument could have just awakened his pain for rage to take over. I don't think anything I shared was big news.

"Since I'm sharing. Whittaker Tate said that he would consider Margaux or Yates Aldrich, Merritt's big rival, as primo suspects."

"Thanks, Margaux was my first suspect. But Yates Aldrich is new for me, too. I'll look into him." He turned to go.

"Yates is staying at the casino hotel near here. I may or may not be having dinner there tonight with my boyfriend. If we should bump into Mr. Aldrich, I'll gladly tell you all about it."

Detective Sullivan turned to face me again. His steely eyes bore into mine. "The manager here tells me you work with hotel security where you're from and even have assisted with murder investigations. So I let you sit in, and I didn't interfere last night with Tate. But I don't want you getting in over your head. Frankly, I'm surprised Tate even spoke to you. But I don't know anything about Aldrich, and I don't need a civilian getting hurt in the middle of my investigation."

I considered what he said. He didn't *forbid* me from going tonight. "I'll be careful and my boyfriend, who hires out as a bodyguard, will be with me every moment."

Sullivan leaned toward me until his face was inches

from mine, "Your boyfriend had better never leave your side and be as good as you think he is."

He turned and strode out of the room, taking the air with him. Mason was as good as I thought he was. I'd seen him in action several months ago. He was former marine special forces sniper class in firearms, Black belt 4th degree Marine Corps martial arts, and black belt 5th degree TaeKwonDo. Mason was a weapon all by himself. But all that doesn't stop a speeding arrow.

I was properly chastised.

I stayed in the room and turned my phone back on. I had missed a call from Beverly; she wanted to discuss the research she had sent me. Blast, I hadn't read through it yet. I might as well call her back now. I didn't know when I would return to training the front desk girls.

Beverly had sent me a Zoom link, so I sent a text that I was available and clicked the link. Within a few moments, Beverly joined. She was on her back patio at the townhome complex where we both live. There were potted and hanging plants everywhere, creating a little tropical oasis on her compact back patio. She was looking lively in her purple blouse with a rhinestone broach and a red hat atop her snow white hair. It must be time for her monthly Red Hat Society meeting.

"Beverly, I'm sorry. I haven't read through everything yet. But I will, really." I said.

"I hadn't read through everything that I sent you either. But this morning I was skimming through some articles I'd sent you and found something significant." Her eyebrows bopped up and down.

"Okay, what it is. Hit me." I joked along.

"The Howell Venture Capital Firm's CFO, that's Chief Financial Officer, is Preston Richards. Guess what sport he is active in and quite good at? Go ahead, guess." She was bubbly and bouncy.

I was never a big sports person. For it to be of any relevance to this case, it could only be one thing.

"Are you telling me Preston shoots with a bow and arrow? Like in a competition or something?" I held my breath.

"Oh, better than competition shooting where it is a fixed target. He *hunts* with it and has bagged big game with a fancy compound bow. He's serious about it." She may be onto something.

"What does the article say?"

"Says he began bow hunting with his father as a teen and that he has become well known in the bow hunting community. Does this help?" She was busy checking her plants to see if they needed watering.

"Beverly, you are a researching wiz. Yes, it helps a lot. Thank you!" I said.

She smiled brightly as we said goodbye.

Margaux had pointed suspicion at Preston. I thought back to my conversation with her out on the smoking veranda. She said Merritt had seduced Preston's wife and that Preston must have found out because they were no longer as close as before. She claimed Merritt said he wished Preston wasn't attending this executive retreat.

Seems I really needed to chat up Preston Richards. I left the suite and looked in Connor's room for Graciella. I couldn't even get close because the forensics team had arrived and were going over every inch of the room. If Connor were guilty, something would turn up in his room.

I phoned Graciella, but it went to her voicemail. She was probably scrambling to catch up on her cleaning schedule. I found Maria at the front desk again.

She spoke before I even got a chance to, "How is the investigation in Connor's room going?"

"It's in full force, but I don't know what they may find."

"Don't worry about the training. Audrey said we would try again tomorrow. I think the new boss called again, so you're probably going to be focused on this situation first." She shrugged.

"Since you mentioned it, I need to talk to Preston

Richards of the group. Know him?" I crossed my fingers and toes.

"Yeah, actually he is the only one I actually like to deal with. He is polite." She narrowed her eyes, "You don't think he…"

"Well, maybe. But I would like to see what he has to say. Any chance he takes his lunch away from the group or something? I'd like to talk to him sooner rather than later."

"You're in luck. When you guys got Connor out of the meeting, Preston slipped out barely a minute later. He is at the outdoor pool enjoying more than a few spiked drinks from what I hear."

"Looks like I need a little sun. Can you ask a landscaper or maintenance guy to keep an eye on me while I talk to him? Just to be on the safe side." She agreed.

I raced to my room and changed for the pool. Since I was representing the new owner on this trip, my swimsuit was a one piece with just a little sexiness to it for Mason's benefit. I hoped Preston had drank just enough spiked drinks to loosen his tongue and talk to an attentive female.

I slowed down to a sedate walk once I was outside. There was a slight breeze and today it was only one hundred in the shade. Potted palm trees surrounded the outdoor pool. It was large and divided into two sections. The closer section had a rock structure for water to cascade down. The other half was on the back side of the rock mound and had lanes for more structured swimming. There were two men and three women swimming in the lanes and a few couples splashing about in the more casual side.

I spotted a forty-something skinny, balding, and pasty white guy in shorts and a tee-shirt reclining in a lounge chair with an umbrella. He would probably turn as red as a lobster if exposed to the sun for more than a minute. That had to be the top finance guy. And the lounge chair next to him was empty. *Not for long.*

I strode up and acted like I was choosing a spot, then I spread my towel over the lounge chair and took my place next to Preston Richards. There were only eight sunning themselves, so it was obvious when I sat next to him rather than one of the dozen empty chairs.

I looked around and spotted a landscaper tending some Bougainvillea plants in the surrounding flowerbeds. *Okay, I had backup. Showtime.*

But I hadn't thought up how to start a conversation ahead of time. I settled in and laid back against the lounge chair. What to say? How do I break the ice?

A server came around and asked Preston if he wanted another lemonade. Preston noticed I was paying attention to his exchange with the bartender, "Would you like a libation, miss?" Maria was correct, he was polite.

"I'll have whatever he's having." Hoping this was my way into a conversation with him.

"So, it's my turn. I don't know if I should feel left out or honored that you spared me til now. I rather enjoy a calm conversation by the pool with a lovely young lady, though. Much more civilized, I think." His thin lips smiled, but his eyes were cunning and evaluating.

"I know you're Preston, the CFO. I'm Julienne, I represent the new owner of the resort and I'm just helping for a little during the transition phase."

"Julienne, nice to meet you." He stopped talking while the bartender sat our drinks down on the little table between us. Preston extracted a travel size bottle of liquor from his pocket, added some to his drink, then offered the bottle to me. I declined.

"Now, what brings you to me?" He asked, then took a gulp from his drink.

This was going far easier than I expected. Apparently, everyone knew I was asking questions.

"Well, sir --"

"Call me Preston, none of this 'sir' stuff."

"Okay, Preston. It's come to my attention that Merritt allegedly... um, seduced your wife." I was uncomfortable with blurting it out in such a harsh way. Yeah, I'm such a hard core investigator, I choke when infidelity comes up.

Preston's forehead creased and his mouth clenched into a thin line. "Somebody actually said such a thing?" He let out a huff of air, "Just when I thought this group couldn't shock me any further, I find they are worse than I gave them credit."

"You must admit, that is a powerful motive. Even if it was just an argument at first. I imagine Merritt wasn't an easy person to work for under the best of circumstances." I had seen on television, interrogators built rapport with the suspect. It was worth a try.

"We used to be good friends. I was one of the first hires with the company, and we had a sort of trenches bond at first. But Merritt changed. His entire ethical compass mutated, and he wasn't the same person. He became amoral, and all that mattered was his advancement, his pleasure, his desires, and his wealth. I no longer knew him." He grabbed a bottle of sunscreen and slathered it on his legs.

"Are you saying it isn't true?" I might as well press since he was talking. No pain, no gain.

"I'm saying I'm shocked somebody would even suggest such a thing. My wife and I have never gotten into the gutter with the others. We often leave any gatherings early and put distance between ourselves and the others at parties. It's just not who either of us are." He moved to smearing some on his arms.

"Is that a yes or no?" I pushed.

"I'm saying it's a lie, complete and utter garbage." He huffed.

"What about the falling out you two had? What was it over?" The words had barely left my mouth when he paled. That was saying something since he was pasty to begin with. He paused for a second, then continued his smearing.

"I can't discuss what we disagreed on, that is sensitive company information. You understand. It wasn't anything to kill him over, if that is what you're thinking." He looked at me sideways, then coated his face with sunscreen.

"What I wonder is that Merritt was killed with an arrow and you seem to have quite the reputation with a bow and arrow. Plus, you had that falling out and were no longer close. You say it was over some confidential business information, but it could have been over the affair he reportedly had with your wife." I shrugged a shoulder.

"Ah, it would appear I'm a prime suspect then. But I say again that you have a false premise that Merritt seduced my wife, somehow. Without that, what is my motive, pray tell?" His voice was even, cold. Underneath his politeness was a shrewd man, perhaps even manipulative, I was guessing.

"For the sake of argument, if Merritt didn't sleep with your wife, then it would follow the estrangement between you was about something else. Even if that was business related, it was enough to drive a wedge between the two of you. I posit that the source of the coolness between you could be compelling enough to use your unique talents to kill the insufferable man." I leaned closer to him and whispered, "Since you're in finance, could it have to do with the company's books?"

His eyes flashed larger, "You are fishing, my dear. I won't rise to your bait."

"Oh, but you did. So, it was something financial. You took it up with Merritt, which makes me wonder if he was part of the financial issue. Am I right?"

"What I will tell you is that Connor was waging full out war on Merritt. Besides Margaux being his longest lasting conquest, Connor gave Merritt deliberately bad advice and then publicly denounced the moves as uninformed. Merritt gave back just as much sabotage, too. I said several times those two would come to blows. Perhaps Connor jumped directly to killing him and put the blame on me by using a bow and arrow." He said.

He stood and smiled a tight phony smile, "You'll have to excuse me. I'm too fair skinned to be in the sun any longer. I'm glad my interrogation is over. Good day." He picked up his sunscreen and drink and walked back to the resort door.

I'm no expert in micro-expressions or body language, but I believed he thought it impossible for

Merritt to have swayed his wife away from her wedding vows. He certainly reacted to my mention of a financial issue involving Merritt and he had said all that mattered to Merritt was his advancement, his pleasure, his desires, and his wealth and that he became amoral. What if Merritt was being dishonest and skimming money from investors somehow? That would be very sensitive information that Preston wouldn't want disclosed to just anyone and have federal auditors descend on the company. But he wouldn't want to go to jail for something Merritt had done either. I imagine that would ruin a friendship and breed resentment, but would he kill over it?

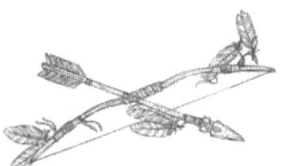

CHAPTER 9

I jumped up and went to my room. After changing back into my work clothes, essentially an azure pant suit with sensible shoes, I went to the offices. I got the green light to do a few hours of training with the front desk girls since the three of them were working today just for scheduled training. The little cafe was open, and I bought a healthy turkey wrap for lunch. I managed three hours of going over the guest services side of the software, then gave them a few quick exercises to practice. Then, I gave them each a sheet with the practice website, including their individual practice login credentials and the assigned homework.

By the time I was done, I felt like I had been going for a few days like the battery bunny on commercials.

The phone vibrated in my blazer pocket. Graciella was calling. I had to admit she was dogged in her duty to call me, and I appreciated her contacting me first this morning. I walked to the empty lobby lounge to answer.

"How are you doing?" Not my usual hello, but she had seemed fairly shaken up over finding the bow.

"I'm okay, thanks for asking." She seemed a little timid, though.

"What's wrong?" I said.

"Um, well… I think somebody on the staff is sharing everything we do regarding the murder with a guest, maybe several guests." She blurted out.

I plopped down into a chair. That would explain Preston's comments about getting around to him, how the venture capital group all knew I was talking to people. That revelation would've been sometime after I talked with Margaux because she thought I was trying to gather gossip to repeat to other hired help.

That might also account for somebody barricading me in the sauna to scare me off. Was the killer paying a staff person for information, or after several years as a guest here had made an ally on the staff. I could see such an ally coming in handy to gather what coworkers were thinking or planning, alliances being forged they thought were under the radar. Yes, an ally on the staff seemed exactly like Merritt, Connor, and even Preston. I didn't think Margaux would bother fostering an ally on the staff.

"What makes you think somebody is leaking information?" I might as well get as much information as I could.

"I heard a few of the wives talking. One of them asked if the informant knew who you were going to interrogate next." Graciella wasn't happy about this, as if the person were giving the resort a bad name.

Working at a luxury resort required a lot of discretion, and this was crossing a line of loyalty to the resort. But this staff person could have fed information to the killer about my mild questions to suspects. No matter how I turned the situation over, this wasn't good for the resort or myself.

"Do you have any idea who this informant might be?" I held my breath.

"Oh, no ma'am. But I'll kick that dog when I find out." Some venom seeped into her voice.

"Do you have others you trust absolutely on staff, maybe two people, who could help you listen and look for who it might be? No questions or following, just eyes and ears open for me." I stressed the last part. Now that we knew, maybe it would become obvious to a coworker.

"Yes ma'am, I have the perfect two who can be eyes and ears with me. We'll start pronto." She hung up. I assumed there was no other gossip or news to report.

I sat in the lobby chair and stared out the window, thinking over the day. I realized that Tiffany was in the parking lot. She was pacing, or perhaps waiting for someone. Oh boy, here we go again. If she thought circumventing me by ambushing Mason was going to work, she really didn't know him at all.

I saw Mason's SUV pull in and park. Tiffany strutted over to him with a big smile on her face. From my vantage point, Mason seemed to scowl at her as she approached and he unloaded his photography gear. She stood in his way and to my surprise he didn't push her aside, just continued what he was doing as if she weren't there. He locked the SUV's doors and motioned for her to step aside. She didn't move, but seemed to be talk fast and almost pleading from what I could see. Mason backed up and went around the cars, but she met him at the door. I wasn't getting in the middle of this. Besides, I wanted to see how he handled this. Mason juggled his equipment to open the door, and I could hear her speaking in a soothing tone as they entered.

"Look, all I'm saying is give me another chance. That's all. If it doesn't work out, I'll understand." She was trailing behind him.

He walked directly to the front desk, "I'd like to speak to security please, right now."

Teresa, who I had just trained, picked up the phone briefly.

Tiffany kept babbling on about second chances. It hadn't been all bad together, and so on. She reached out to touch his arm, and he jerked away.

I was mesmerized, like a car wreck you can't stop watching. Mason was angry, but seemed to keep it under control. One of the security guys appeared and Mason lodged his complaint of harassment and asked that they keep her away from him, like move her to a hotel in town. Mason left while security dealt with her.

The security person took Tiffany aside and solemnly instructed her she couldn't harass other guests or they would have to insist she leave. I slipped unnoticed to the elevator.

I entered our room and Mason spun around, as if Tiffany had followed him. The anger in his eyes softened, and he swept me up in his arms and kissed me passionately. He smelled of the outdoors, rugged and fresh. I felt like I was in a movie, every thought left my mind and I melted into him. I believe this is what "being swept off your feet" must feel like.

We parted, foreheads touching and breathless.

"If this is how you resolve your anger, it's quite stimulating."

"You saw that?" He asked.

I nodded slightly.

"I'm sorry somebody from my past is haunting us and ruining our time."

"I'm not. A girl wonders how her beau will handle temptation, a pretty girl throwing herself at him. I get to see firsthand how you protect what we have. I wish it wasn't happening, but I am choosing to see the good." Sure, I had every right to be furious, but it wouldn't do any good. We weren't perfect, we had issues like any couple, we both had baggage, but this showed more than words that he wasn't a player anymore and he's serious about our relationship. That made my insides flutter. My knees were barely holding me up from the kiss as it was.

Mason wore slim cut faded jeans and a tee shirt for his wilderness photography hiking. He looked disheveled, manly, and a pinch disreputable. I wondered if we would order room service, but Mason pulled away.

"I'll jump in the shower and get ready for our night at the casino." He gave me a peck on the cheek, "But if this Yates Aldrich makes any moves on you, I may go all martial arts on him."

"I forgive you in advance." Drat, I had forgotten all about the casino tonight. It looked as though we wouldn't get intimate time until the murder was solved or perhaps when we got home.

I surveyed my wardrobe choices. I had one slightly more dressy outfit, a little black dress. It took some searching with Felicia to find one that wasn't short but right at the kneecap. I never felt comfortable in short skirts, especially when my work image was involved. I had aspirations for management, and you never knew what could hurt your reputation. The black dress was a one piece sheath in a knit jersey with a draped neckline and sleeveless and it hugged my hips but flared a smidge from there down. It was comfortable and light-weight for the summer heat while being appropriate for a night out.

Mason dressed in smoky grey slacks and blazer with a peach colored button-down shirt open a few buttons. I love a man who knows how to dress up. I would have skipped tonight at the slightest suggestion from Mason, but I suspected he was enjoying helping me. He also knew I would go looking for Mr. Aldrich my first chance if we didn't go tonight. I would much rather he be by my side.

The resort had three casinos and was a twenty-minute drive and just off highway 285. It was adobe Spanish Mission style on the outside, but sleek. It was big, with five stories that wrapped like a horseshoe around to the back. In the front courtyard stood a massive bronze statue of a Native American dancing.

Walking into the resort part of this entertainment complex was overwhelming. Inside the floors were marble and polished granite rather than the red Spanish tile. The lobby had a soaring open high ceiling with large blond pine logs that radiated out like spokes in a wheel on the ceiling. Everywhere you looked was Native American artwork ranging from modern to traditional, plus pottery in glass displays. I am used to European elegance at my home resort where I work, so this was a style of luxury I hadn't experienced before and it was impressive.

We made our way to the Wild Sage restaurant. Mason's hand was on my back as we walked, but we both swiveled our heads, looking for Mr. Yates Aldrich. A forty something man with honey brown hair styled with spiked tufts and a trimmed short beard. That was all I knew from what I looked up on my cell phone.

The restaurant was ultra modern with lots of natural brick, dark wood on the floor and tables, and a minimalist approach. By the time we reached our table, I had scanned the other diners and didn't see anybody resembling Aldrich's description.

I doubted we would happen across him in the massive complex. We chatted about the photos Mason had been taking on his daily forays over Guacamole made table side. I was looking forward to seeing his work and considered myself lucky to be the first to enjoy them.

I feasted on the Baja Fish Tacos and Mason devoured the short-rib enchiladas. We tried a new-for-us cocktail, the Paloma; tequila, gran marnier, a splash of grapefruit juice, topped off with grapefruit soda served in red clay handleless mugs. The Palomas were a refreshing, summery libation that I drank down after the heat of the walk from the parking lot.

After dinner we meandered around the resort and found the casino. I made mental notes of all the interesting ways this resort did various things differently that are invisible to guests such as tactics for traffic flow. Once in the casino, we strolled to the Blackjack table where Mr Tate claimed to have seen Aldrich. There was no sign of anyone that could be Aldrich. Mason and I stood back out of the way and looked around, as if deciding what we wanted to play.

Mason motioned his head to indicate another section with several poker tables behind glass. It appeared players were just arriving and there was Aldrich, just like the photo online. Mason led me to the registration table where a young man and woman registered players.

Mason addressed the man, "Hello, I'd like to join. What's the buy in?"

"Tonight is fifty dollar buy in for no-limit hold 'em. You get five thousand starting chips and twenty-minute blind levels. If you bust out before the end of the first hour, there is a one-time fifty dollar re-buy," He said.

Mason paid his fifty dollars to the man, "If she's not playing, your girlfriend will have to watch from the other side of the glass."

I bit my lip. I knew Mason had played high stakes poker before, and according to what I read online after I first met him and looked him up, he was considered a skilful player. He won a handful of tournaments. I had nothing to worry about. This wasn't Vegas, he wouldn't lose everything he owned. Still, I was nervous over the idea. But this might be a great way to talk to Aldrich after the game without my being dangled as a carrot.

On the other side of the glass, a few people joined me to watch. After the first few hands were played, my feet were tired. I stopped a server leaving the poker room after getting the players drinks and asked for bottled water.

"Are you with one of the players?" She asked. I nodded and pointed Mason out. "You can get a mixed drink free since you're with a player." I upgraded to a margarita and bottled water.

One of the lady bystanders overheard, "You might

wanna get a chair if you're planning on waiting. They're just getting started."

"How long do these things go?" I couldn't help but sound ignorant about Mason's world of gambling.

"I believe tonight's only four hours. You're lucky it isn't one of the seven hour or longer games."

I watched for a half hour and then played some slot machines. I cashed in my two-hundred and fifty dollars and went back to watching the game. The players had decreased by half.

"How's that guy doing?" I asked a guy watching.

"Oh, he's good. Of these players I think he and that guy," he pointed to Aldrich, "are the best players. It'll be interesting to see which one wins." He never looked away from the players. Another watcher tapped me on the shoulder and pointed up above the glass windows to a closed circuit television broadcasting the game. It was from above, looking down on the table without showing individual hands. I dragged a chair over and settled in for the duration.

Aldrich and Mason were well matched, or so it seemed. I wouldn't know if Mason was holding back to get Aldrich's attention or fighting for his life. His expression gave away nothing. Looking at Mason play, he exuded a serious aura. I hadn't been able to picture him as a marine until now. His demeanor was all business and whatever it took to get the job done, he would do. I knew he didn't like being in the military; it didn't fit his artistic soul, and he did it more because his father was a general and expected him to join. But I was willing to bet my winnings he was a good Marine.

The game finally finished after four hours, with Aldrich winning the most and Mason in second. I watched as Mason shook his hand and they began chatting. Mason motioned to me and broken away, at which point Aldrich joined him and talked some more. They came out the door together and joined me. Aldrich was in a tailored suit that looked expensive and ostentatious.

"Julienne, this is Yates Aldrich. Yates, this is Julienne," he still wore his poker face, so I knew this was all part of a plan.

Aldrich took over the conversation, "I insisted we have a drink together before you two take off."

A few minutes later I was seated in the Squash Blossom lounge enjoying a cocktail seated between Mason and Aldrich. Since I was stuck next to Aldrich, I removed a stickpin with a lovely enamel gecko on one end and a two-inch needle on the other that had been adorning my dress. I kept it ready in case I needed it. I ran over different scenarios of how to move the conversation to the murder.

"Where are you two staying?" His eyes on me.

"We're staying at the Enchantment Canyon Resort. It's a beautiful oasis, but we wanted to check out the restaurant here." I didn't want to be the silent girlfriend who couldn't speak for herself.

"Their food is a bit too healthy for me, too. I like a bit of indulgence and spice." Again he was talking to me. I felt Mason stiffen next to me. Oh boy, we'd be lucky to get out of here with Aldrich still breathing if he kept this up.

"So, you've been there before. How about this visit, did you visit Enchantment Canyon for old time's sake?" I tried to keep my voice conversational.

His eyes changed for a second; narrowed and took on an edge for the briefest flash. "No, not this trip. I've seen it once, and that was enough for me." He tried a smoldering look. Mason's smoldering look is the one that turns my knees to jello. This guy's made my skin crawl. *Eeew, women actually fell for this sleazy act.* I took a gulp of my drink.

Now what? How to bring up Merrit and the murder? I glanced at Mason, but I couldn't read him in his poker-face mode.

Oh what the heck, "Yates Aldrich, you're a big competitor of Howell Venture Capital, right? I guess you've heard about his sudden death." I watched his reaction.

He leaned back and crossed his arms and looked us both up and down. "What's going on here?"

Mason answered, "We just want to ask you who you

think might've killed him?" Mason met my eyes, and I understood he wanted to get him talking first before we peppered him with our questions.

"And why would I talk to you about his death?" He asked.

"The resort wants this resolved quickly, so we're helping. Anything you share could help us." Mason answered again, which was fine by me. I may not want to be silent, but I also didn't want much attention from sleazy guys.

"Okay. I think Preston Richards, the CFO, is the guy you should look at." He stayed back in his seat with his arms crossed. Completely defensive.

"Why Preston? I've heard he was good friends with Merritt." I managed to say without flinching when he looked at me, making me feel dirty.

"I hear Preston was distressed about some shady things Merritt had done that could get the entire company sanctioned by the Securities and Exchange Commission." He leaned forward and uncrossed his arms.

"Can you be more specific about these shady things?" Mason leaned forward as well.

"I don't know the details, but Preston contacted me about a job. It was really laughable. In this age of corporate espionage, I wasn't about to trust Merritt's lapdog."

He looked at me and I felt his hand on my knee, then sliding up my thigh, "I might remember more with the proper motivation," He said.

Mason tensed and was likely close to punching Yates.

My surprise wore off fast. I held my stick pin firmly as I stabbed it into his hand, trying to avoid my thigh. He let out several curses as he withdrew his hand. I was happy to see I had drawn blood. He glared at me.

"It was that, or I let this former Marine take you behind the resort to one of the loading docks," I calmly said with a smile, even though I was shaken by his actions. He acted as if he were entitled.

"I still might." Mason snarled.

"I may contact security and report you." I added.

"Like they'll believe you over my word." He snarled, holding a napkin over his wound.

"Considering I work in resort security myself, I think they'll believe me." He didn't need to know I didn't work at this resort.

His face turned red, and he jumped up, knocking his chair backwards. Mason jumped up to meet any trouble he may cause, but Yates Aldrich stomped out.

I noticed the entire lounge was quiet and everyone was watching us.

I held up the stickpin, "Some men have to learn the

hard way to keep their hands to themselves." I smiled sweetly.

A woman at one table yelled out, "Amen, sister." Several women clapped, nodding. I gave a little bow before we left, Mason threw enough money on the table to cover drinks and tip.

CHAPTER 10

*I*t was late, and I was exhausted, as I imagined so was Mason. I don't know how he managed the early morning and long travel to his photo spots, then dinner and a four-hour poker tournament. Then the adrenaline rush of a near fist fight.

We discussed the suspects to keep alert on the drive.

Connor wanted to take over the company, and perhaps Merritt Howell didn't like his wife sleeping with the enemy. We agreed the karma of Connor doing to Merritt what he had done to Whittaker Tate was ironic.

Margaux and Connor alibied each other, but she was a suspect too. She had said it was like being freed from a tormentor. I still didn't know if she inherited Merritt's money or any interest or shares in the company.

Mason and I agreed Preston was the top suspect. He had a falling out with Merritt, probably over some illegal shenanigans. The unlikely scenario, as far as I was concerned, was Merritt seducing Preston's wife as a motive. I hadn't actually met her, but I believed Preston thought it was inconceivable, so that wasn't a motive. But most damning of all, he hunted with a bow and arrow.

Whittaker Tate, who lost everything because of Merritt, claimed he let go of all the anger and went to forgive Merritt for his wife's suicide? I think he was second on my list after Preston. I couldn't just get over such an underhanded and vile treatment.

Then there was sordid Yates Aldrich. He's Merritt's biggest competitor and rival. Plus, they supposedly hated each other. In addition, Merritt may have staked his flag on Yates' wife and made the competition too personal. I never got to ask Aldrich about his wife and Merritt. What was with these successful men unable to be faithful in marriage?

I turned and studied Mason. I believed he was finished with being a Don Juan. He honestly wanted to be faithful, I believed. I wanted to tell him how I valued that, but I couldn't find the words.

"I'm glad you aren't like Aldrich or Merritt." Clumsy, but I got it out.

"I'm glad I'm not like them anymore. I grew up

and realized having one woman for the rest of my life was what I really want and value. I've found that in you, and I am lucky beyond words."

We parked and walked, holding hands, into the resort. I enjoyed holding hands, call me corny. A quiet hung over the lobby and halls like a tomb. A bad feeling settled in my stomach. I stopped at the front desk.

"How is everything tonight?" I asked the young man, Juan, according to his nametag.

"Quiet, almost too quiet." He said and glanced around.

I turned and felt a wave of cold wash over me. The front entrance door was closed and the air conditioning didn't create cold spots. *Odd*.

Mason and I collapsed into bed, too tired for any extra-curricular activity. There was a loud thump against the door when I was just drifting into slumber's waiting arms. I looked over at Mason to find him fully asleep. I debated going to look and decided I should since I worked for the company.

I slipped on a light robe and peered through the peephole. I saw the tip of a foot sticking out into the hall, as if a person were sitting against my door. Was the man drunk? I opened the door slowly. The man was sitting with his back against my door with an arrow sticking out of his chest. It was Preston Richards, staring blankly ahead.

"Mason, we have a problem." I called out.

In order to look out the door for anybody fleeing this gruesome tableau, I opened the door wider and let Preston hit the floor. His head made a thunk. Nobody was in the hall.

Mason was beside to me in a flash. He held me in one arm while calling the front desk on his cell phone.

I shook from the shock. Mason angled me so I wasn't looking right at Preston. Why would the killer dump the body at my door? Was it meant to scare me? My chief suspect was dead, and I felt like I was pointedly told to back off.

The night security person arrived at a run. Little more than a kid himself, he looked like he could handle parking tickets rather than stare death in the face. He gulped several times as he looked down at the body. He looked up at us as if we needed to explain ourselves for the dead man across our threshold.

"I already called the police." Mason informed him.

"What happened here?" His voice wavered a bit.

"I heard something hit the door. When I opened it, he was propped against it." I answered in a stronger voice than his. Not that I felt any more confident, but sadly this wasn't my first close encounter with a dead body.

"Why don't you go wait for the police to arrive?" Mason suggested.

"Oh, I can't leave the body alone now. Evidence might be removed." He said while looking us over.

"Fine, then I'm going down to meet them." I wrapped my robe tighter around me as if it were a talisman to ward off evil and strode out.

It took the police fifteen minutes to arrive and another five minutes before Detective Sullivan arrived, hair mussed and yawning. I hoped he wouldn't hold me responsible for disturbing his sleep.

"These two are the guests in this room. They claim they didn't do it." The security boy said while eyeing Mason and I. I was guessing he didn't know I worked with the new owner of the resort, or maybe he just didn't care.

"Ms. LaMere, Mr. Sheridan," he nodded to us. "Let's step inside and talk." Once we were away from the door, he took our statements.

"So neither of you saw anyone in the hall?" We shook our heads no.

He pursed his lips, "Seems somebody wasn't finished in their mission and made your lives more interesting." He scrutinized us both, "You say you were just getting back from being out. Mind telling me where you were and what you were doing there?"

Mason answered for us, "We were at the Resort and Casino off the hiway. We had a wonderful dinner, then I played in one of the casino's poker tournaments. We

had a drink afterward and then came back here."
Simple. Nothing unusual about our night. We are not the culprit you are looking for.

Detective Sullivan squinted at us and didn't move for a full minute. Finally he said, "You two need to be more forthcoming with me, right now. This is two people dead now, and I know this feisty filly has been asking questions."

Mason and I exchanged a look, I nodded my accent to him. "Okay, Detective. We went looking for Mr. Yates Aldrich, a bitter rival of Howell's, and we found him. I played cards with him and we had a drink and chatted him up after the game. He seemed to think that Mr. Richards on the floor over there was the most likely to kill Merritt Howell." I was fine with Mason doing the talking in the hopes the detective would take the news better from a man. You know how that goes, ladies.

"I looked you two up. While you may be highly trained, and even considered deadly in your own right Mr. Sheridan, you both are in over your heads. As for you, Ms. LaMere, I talked to a Detective Johan Larson of your local police. Apparently you assisted the Vail police this last winter. He said you were a quasi informant of sorts for him. Larson tells me you could be useful." He paused, and I waited for the "but." "On the one hand, you might be helpful, but on the other hand you could be in further danger, be killed, or seriously hurt."

I raised a finger rather than a hand, requesting to speak. He nodded for me to speak my mind. "I'm also part of the security team at my home resort, thus the owner is expecting me to assist. This second murder will have him pressuring me even harder. I propose I have another security person or Mason with me at all times for the remainder of my stay here, allowing me to ask a few more questions safely."

He let out a long-suffering sigh. "I'll go along with that, but you must share everything you learned with me now."

He took out his phone, recorded what each suspect shared with me. "I hadn't gotten that far. I'm not sure why the killer would leave the prime suspect at my door."

Detective Sullivan shook his head slowly, "I have to admit, you've gotten more from their back stabbing than I have from formal interviews. You just saved me significant time. I expect you to call me with each piece of new information. Understood?"

I nodded, "Understood. Absolutely."

By the time the detective left and the body was removed, it was three in the morning. We collapsed in bed, again. Mason was instantly asleep, but my mind kept churning over the events and suspects. Why kill Merritt Howell and then Preston Richards?

"Mr. Carlton has already called. Apparently, the Howell Venture Capital CFO's murder after the CEO's murder is all over the business news this morning. He wants to talk to you, immediately." Audrey informed me as soon as I reported for work. Her eyes looked at me with part worry and part fear. I felt for her. A transition to a new owner was stressful, but then to have a killer on the premises really gets the instincts screaming to run away.

I was functioning, if you could call it that, on just three hours of fitful sleep. My eyes felt like a sandpit in a sandstorm, and I had a hefty headache setting up camp at the base of my skull. I had already dealt with my entire family calling about second murder. My father was ready to fly down and take over as per his usual reaction. I might as well get the call with Mr. Carlton over with. I expected he would call, and I was pretty sure he wouldn't be happy with my not magically fixing the situation already.

Audrey let me use her office to make the call. Her office was about the size of mine back home. It allowed me just enough room to pace. I think she knew Mr. Carlton wasn't going to tread lightly on my feelings. His secretary put my call right through, oh goody!

"Julienne, we are at Defcon 4. I don't have to tell

you that this is the worst possible time for a resort to have such adverse publicity. A transition has inherent difficulties melding two cultures and outlooks into one and there is a risk of losing loyal customers." He took a breath and reloaded, "But this sort of attention on top of the resort being under new ownership could devastate its brand and loyal base for years to come. I'm told you were attempting a subtle approach to keep customers from getting ruffled feathers. But that approach is out the door. Understand?" His voice boomed in through my head.

"Yes, sir. No more subtle questioning." I just repeated, no sense arguing. My head couldn't take it, anyway.

"I have arranged to bring any suspects to you throughout the day to question them. Get to the bottom of this! I want you coordinating with the local police, too."

"I've been sharing information with the lead detective on the case already, sir." At least I had that box checked before he could accuse me of not making any headway at all.

Even though I had expected Mr. Carlton to pressure me, I had a rock in my stomach. I felt the weight of the transition's success being placed squarely on my shoulders. I walked to a wall and rested my head against it as I listened to him lecture me even more. By the time he hung up, I felt like crying. *Buck up LaMere, your physically drained, and the pressure is making you emotional. You got this. Yeah, sure.*

I stayed with my head against the cool plastered wall for a few minutes. I could only do my best. Right now, that was just taking one step after another. Clearly I wouldn't be training anymore until the killer was in police custody. If Mr. Carlton arranged for me to question suspects, I had better find out what that looked like.

I opened Audrey's office door to find Audrey, Jonathan, and Carlos standing outside waiting for me. Audrey winced when she saw me. I must look quite a sight.

Jonathan took the lead, "Did he make you cry?"

My eyebrows bunched together in response.

"Your eyes are all red and puffy, dear." Audrey shared. "She looked like that before the call." She told the others.

"Oh, practically no sleep, and now I'm to fix this nightmare, somehow. That's all." I added.

Carlos stepped forward, "I'm here to assist you in any manner you need. I've set up a room for you to meet with people and talk privately. Just tell me who you want and I will collect them quietly." They all stood looking at me. I wasn't sure how to proceed. I still hadn't gone over the research Beverly had sent me, and I felt I needed to do that to prepare for anything more.

"Tell you what, I have some research to read on my suspects to prepare for questioning. Let's start with Whittaker Tate and Yates Aldrich in about an hour." I gave where they were each staying to contact them and invite them to speak with me. Jonathon revealed the interview room was the guest library, where the bow and arrow had been on display. Seemed fitting, actually. I would have the vengeful brave's tale there to inspire me.

I returned to my room and looked for the slip of paper Maria had given me just the other day for Miguel RunningElk, the man who told the story of the vengeful brave's legend. I finally found it in the pocket of my pants where I had put it the other day.

It rang and rang until an old-fashioned answering machine picked up, "This is Miguel and Consuella, you know what to do." After the beep, I left my message to please call me.

"Hello Mr. RunningElk. I am working at the Enchantment Canyon Resort and would like to talk to you about the bow and arrow that were on display and the accompanying legend of the Native American brave." I left my name and cell phone number before hanging up.

It still bothered me that Merritt's last words were about a curse. Why did he think a curse got him?

I turned on my laptop and sat down a cold mango juice drink from the cafe, making myself comfortable at the round table by the sliding doors. My room overlooked a side of the resort with the desert stretching out with cactus and yucca plants.

I found the email Beverly sent with information copied into the text and several links to articles. Since I wasn't a fast reader, I might get halfway through everything before the interviews. I looked for anything on Tate and Aldrich to prepare for meeting with them.

Aldrich was in one article about Merritt Howell. Merritt credited his competition with Aldrich as what continually spurred him on to bigger and greater accomplishments. A somewhat backhanded compliment.

There were several links about Tate, but I picked the one in a business journal. It went into how Whittaker Tate was the crucial factor that drove any company success at the venture capital firm since it opened its doors. They credited him with finding investors to match the investments they felt were worthy. He had great business acumen and could spot a startup that could really become successful companies with the proper money and guidance. Tate was the one who would often mentor the fledgling businesses as well. I took a break and drank some of my juice and considered. Tate's abilities and hard work built the company. He made the company successful by ensuring the companies he took under his wing were not just profitable but flourishing. That had to come from his commitment to the *people* in the companies. I went back to reading.

Then Howell began a campaign to take over and systematically tore Tate down to investors and startups alike, getting them to place themselves in Merritt's hands rather than Tate's. By the time Tate was forced to step down, his wife's suicide had torn apart his world The article ended with a bleak outlook for the company without Tate's steady and experienced hand. I didn't have time to read the remaining two articles on Whittaker Tate, but the one would help me question him again. This article didn't mention the exact reason his wife couldn't go on.

My cell phone rang; Graciella.

I barely answered when she began speaking, "I have those company retreat people asking me who you are going to question. Somehow they know I'm giving you information and that you're going to be more formally asking questions on behalf of the resort. I don't know who is blabbing to them, but it isn't good." She was fuming. I could practically feel her anger radiate from my phone.

"Do you have any ideas who might be their informant?"

"No, but I'm sure as h… sure going to find out! I'll let you know when I know who the little blabbermouth is." She hung up. I pitied the person who had to answer to her for being the snitch.

I couldn't worry about her headhunting right now. I was due downstairs in the guest library. I checked my appearance in the mirror. Azure blue power skirt suit with blush blouse and shoes. I picked through my overnight bag and found some eye drops. At least I would look professional and ready to *interview* suspects.

To my incredulity, Yates Aldrich sat in one of the leather chairs waiting. His cologne, Channel Allure if my memory served, was overpowering. He wore a royal blue and white striped polo shirt and coordinated blue shorts, as if he was on his way to a tennis match. Both the shirt and shorts were noticeably snug.

Carlos closed the door, and it was just the three of us. Cozy. I was skeptical at first about Carlos being present, but the lecherous look Mr. Aldrich gave me from my feet to my chest made me grateful for his presence.

"You? You're the new resort owner's representative who wants to talk to me? I thought you worked in security at the resort and casino." He attempted a smoldering look yet again that failed in every way. "Isn't he going to spoil our fun?" He gestured towards Carlos and licked his lips.

"I am the owner's representative and I'll be asking for your help with information that might lead to the murder of two people. Nothing more." I stood looking down on him sitting in the chair.

"I came to help. I'm a helpful citizen." He attempted an innocent look, but that failed as well. *How in blazes was this man successful in business?* He probably did one thing well, hired good people to do the actual work.

I remained standing, "Mr. Aldrich, when we last spoke you were pretty sure that Preston Richards was the likely killer of Merritt Howell." He shifted in his chair. "I understand your relationship with Merritt was more than a bitter personal rivalry. In fact, I was told you hated Merritt. Something about showing your wife what a real man was like." I made that last part up. I needed to get him off his game. "That would make you a prime suspect. The investigating detective expects me to share what I find out, and right now you have the most vehemence toward the late Merritt Howell."

"I didn't kill anybody. And I had nothing against Preston Richards. I had no reason to kill that man. Besides, I already got even with Merritt." He sat on the edge of the chair and leaned forward as if he were sharing a secret. "I got his personal assistant to spy for me. I snatched several excellent companies out from under Merritt and invested in them first. It's far better to destroy somebody's life than merely kill them." He smirked. That was genuine.

"Well, that's what you say now. But I think you were still furious with Merritt for his bedding your wife and using her against you. And then there is the fact that you said Preston came to you for a job and you thought it was a corporate espionage attempt. So, I can see why you would get even with him too. I'm not really seeing an *innocent* man before me. Far from it."

Aldrich licked his lips again, "Look, it could've been any number of husbands or jilted lovers that got even with Merritt." He looked between me and Carlos at the door. "Last night I was in another poker game and then engaged in some physical activity with a girl from the bar." He perked up and added, "I think it's symbolic Merritt was shot through the heart. Right, wasn't it through the heart? Well, there you go. It was revenge for his trampling on somebody's heart."

I scoffed, "You would know something about that yourself from what I was told. Let's see, it was something like you were just as much a vile snake as Merritt, two peas in a pod. Perhaps it's you who finally had your heart broken by Merritt with your wife. You could have paid somebody to remove the problem for you."

"No. No, listen, with Merritt it could be anybody.

He was brutal on the employees once he ran Tate out of the company." His eyes lit up, "Whittaker Tate has got to detest Merritt's guts after everything he put him through. I'm telling you. Tate lost everything and there is nothing more dangerous than a man without something to lose."

I spent a few more minutes trying different approaches, but I didn't seem to get anywhere. I felt like this was such a waste of my time.

What kind of nonsense was the arrow through the heart because he broke someone's heart? Did he think because I was a woman I would fall for such romantic drivel? And looking into a disgruntled employee was something to turn over to the Detective. I sure couldn't track them all and look into each one. At this point, I was ready to believe it was the Native American brave giving two men their justice. But I didn't know why Preston Richards was murdered. Merritt Howell seemed to make enemies rather than friends. Preston seemed hard working and uninterested in scandalous behavior. What did they have in common?

There is nothing more dangerous than a man with nothing to lose. That sentiment rang true.

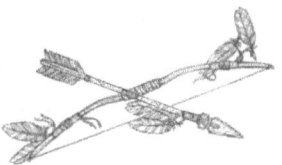

CHAPTER 11

I was barely done considering that thought when Carlos ushered Whittaker Tate in and then closed the doors. His cologne wafted in, Tom Ford's Noir with its spicy yet mellow scent, and he bowed his head in greeting.

I motioned to a chair, and he sat, "What prompted the necessity of my coming here rather than a talk on the phone?" He sat precisely and ran a hand down the crease in his stark white slacks that set off his robin-egg blue polo shirt. Despite his reserved manners, he struck me as a tightly wound spring that would hurt somebody once released.

"I'm sure you've heard the news by now about Preston Richards. Perhaps you could help us with some more insights." I acted as though I was checking my notes. Tate made me nervous by his very presence.

"You had pointed me to Yates Aldrich. I followed up on your suspicion. He claims to have an alibi that I'll check out. What can you tell me about Preston from your time as his boss? Some suggested he killed Merritt… until last night." I was taking a fresh approach with Tate. Not out of sympathy for everything he had been through, rather I sensed he would respond better to respectful conversation.

"Preston was a consummate professional. Came in early to work and stayed late whenever needed. He knew the financials inside and out. For some reason he was friends with Merritt, which never made sense to me. I heard the friendship had some cracks in it over the last few months, though." He sat back, steepled his fingers, and looked at me as if it were my move.

"I believe whoever killed Merritt also killed Preston. What did they have in common? Did they socialize outside of work? Their wives play Bunco together?" I watched him closely but didn't see any sign of emotion. His many years in high finance must have given him nerves of steel and the ability to mask his thoughts.

"The only thing those two had in common was the job, as far as I know. Their wives couldn't relate to each other at all. Preston's wife has a master's degree in French literature, Margaux barely finished high school and thinks spending thousands on Channel clothes makes her a French fashion expert. In another life, I could see Margaux telling the poor to eat cake and being beheaded for it."

"Okay, the job then. What would they both be involved in on the job that could get them killed?" I gave an encouraging small smile.

He let out a sigh, "The company changed after I was run out. The financials in a Venture Capital endeavor are subject to the same laws and scrutiny as any bank making loans. The records must be perfect. Even if there were a problem, it could get them jail time, but not murdered."

"Oh, people have killed for far less." I said.

Whittaker inclined his head, acknowledging my comment, "True. I simply mean, I can't see killing over it when the damage is already done and their deaths wouldn't fix anything."

"Did you have any grief with Preston? Did he side with Merritt when you were destroyed and shoved aside?" I was being a touch more aggressive to see how he'd react.

"I don't believe Preston ever had a hand in Merritt's coup to run me out. Now I'll save you the trouble of dancing around the issue, no I didn't kill Preston or Merritt. I had no issues with Preston."

"Mr. Aldrich was just here a few moments ago, and he tossed a bone to me claiming Merritt treated his employees terribly and perhaps the killer is one of them lurking around the resort and killing them off. What do you think of that idea?"

"I heard rumors that Merritt was putting money before people. But that is common among many, many large corporations and people don't get murdered."

"Can you give me some examples of putting money first? Just so I have an idea." I gave a hint of a smile again.

"I'll give some examples. He fired roughly twenty-five percent of the employees as a *cost cutting* measure and expected the remaining employees to pick up all the slack and yet produce even more. Merritt was getting the name Rambo in Pinstripes. He increased the key man insurance on the executives, he lessened the contributions to retirement 401ks, he cut several other benefits like college reimbursement. All these measures supposedly saved the company millions, but I don't know where that money went. Preston enacted most of those policies. But would an employee kill over these ruthless changes? Doubtful. They would get another job on the sly before Merritt could trash their reputations. Which is exactly what several of his best employees did." He spoke with assurance, this was his comfort zone, talking business.

"Then who do you think was angry enough at both men? Who had been struck such a devastating blow it produced a murderous desire?" I looked him in the eyes, so I caught the slight dawning. Did he think of somebody he believed killed the two men, but he wouldn't share?

"And we are back to thinking I'm the man who lost the most, so I must be the killer? Sorry, I was surrounded by people all last night. I was at my hotel having drinks with a new investor in my own consulting business I've started. I closed the bar down." He stood to go. "Again, I have to say, either Margaux or Yates Aldrich are at the top of my list."

I disliked his deciding the interview was over; it gave him control of the situation. But I had no way to get more information from him, and he was here voluntarily in the first place. I believed he thought of a person who could have an issue with both Merritt and Preston, but kept it to himself.

He swept out of the guest library like a Shake-spearean actor making a dramatic exit, stage left. I let out a sigh. The two men I had just met with were my top picks and they pointed to each other, and the widow. I hadn't gained any more from either man, except the motive to kill both men had to be business related since their private lives didn't intersect. Since I didn't work at Howell Venture, I couldn't imagine what it could be.

Carlos cleared his throat, and I stopped staring into space, "Perhaps a lunch break would give you time to think before meeting with your other two people?" He looked at me with sympathy, and a dash of hope.

"That's a good idea." We arranged for Connor to be the next interviewee after lunch.

I was walking past the lobby on my way to the restaurant and stopped in mid-stride. Outside the front doors, Whittaker Tate stood chatting with Blair. A smile spread on Tate's face, transforming him into a handsome gentleman, and Blair blossomed before my eyes. Her cheeks blazed red in a healthy blush that made her look carefree rather than care worn.

Tate lifted her hand and kissed it, then walked to the parking lot. Blair held her hands up to her cheeks and watched him go. I wanted to see Blair get a happy new life after her husband was sick for so long before dying, but what if Tate was the killer? She deserved better than that.

Blair entered, looking like a teenager who had been asked to the prom by the star quarterback. She saw me watching and blushed brighter.

"I know I'm too old for romance, but that was the nicest surprise I've had in a long while." She giggled, actually giggled. I was waiting for the fluttering hands next.

"Do you know him?" I asked.

"No, I ran into him, not looking where I was going.

Do you know him? Is there something wrong with him?"

"Of course not, I thought maybe you knew him from when you stayed here before. Nothing's wrong." I couldn't bring myself to tell her to go slow or be careful.

"He asked me out, do you believe that? Me! I'm going on a date, at my age." She giggled again.

I had no idea how old she was, particularly now that she was glowing and her eyes were sparkling, but I know she wasn't too old for romance, and maybe a second chance at love.

"Why don't you splurge and go to the spa for a makeover for your date?" I really wanted her to find love. *I had to face it, I was getting sentimental.*

She smiled, showing all her teeth, "That is a lovely idea. I think I'll do that."

I went to the cafe and ate a healthy Kale Caesar salad. I love the resort, and I never felt I was a picky eater, but I enjoyed the cultural meals we had on the plaza and at the casino. The salad was tasty, but it wasn't what I thought of as Santa Fe food.

I sat at my table absorbed in my thoughts about the suspects and my mandate to resolve this. What more could I do to meet Mr. Carlton's expectations of clearing this nightmare up before it hurt the resort's reputation beyond repair? I hadn't read through all the research that Delores sent me, so I could scour through all that research. Maybe something within it would help make sense of the murders since it was likely all business related.

I had a half hour left before I was to question Connor. I didn't expect much cooperation from him. It amazed me that Yates Aldrich and Whittaker Tate had agreed to talk to me at all.

I walked into the library to find a middle-aged man looking at the empty case where the legendary bow and arrow normally were kept.

"I'm sorry to interrupt, I'll leave you alone." I didn't want to chase him away from using the charming library.

"Are you Julienne, the lady who left me a message?" I looked closer at the man. He had tanned skin with wrinkles around his eyes, long hair in a braid down his back, jeans, western shirt, cowboy boots, and a turquoise ring on his finger.

"Mr. RunningElk?" I ventured.

He strode up to me with confidence in his fluid movements and held out his hand, "Pleased to meet you ma'am. I understand you're looking into the situation."

We shook, his hands were rough and calloused, yet gentle.

"I'm doing my best, but I'm not a professional

investigator, so no guarantees." I smiled a weak, apologetic smile. Managing expectations is what that's called, although I felt like that wasn't enough.

"Your best is all that can be asked. But your spirit is eager. I sense a thirst for justice and truth within that pushes you." He motioned to the plaque with the legend of the vengeful brave, "You and the brave of our history have much in common." He cocked his head, his warm chestnut eyes looking into my soul, "Has the brave appeared to you?"

My eyebrows shot up, "Umm, no. He hasn't" I wasn't sure I wanted him to either.

"I sense he is near you. It wouldn't surprise me if his spirit attempts to lend a hand. Look for the signs, follow where the signs lead and you will uncover what you are seeking."

I dropped my gaze to the floor, unsure what to say. "I would be honored for his assistance, I could use it." Which was true. I didn't need to pick apart and evaluate his gesture of goodwill.

I cleared my throat and looked him in the eyes again, "I am hoping you can give me some insight though. I heard Mr. Howell's dying words, and he believed, in that moment, that a curse had gotten him. Can you help me understand that?"

His eyebrows scrunched together, and he considered before answering, "To me it says the legendary brave of local lore appeared to him in some manner showing he was going to pay for his actions that have hurt others." He said, his voice soothing.

"Appeared to him? I wasn't aware of this part of the legend."

"Oh yes, before the legendary brave brings justice to you he appears and warns you. How else will your spirit learn?"

"I see," although I didn't really believe it. "Is there a landmark or specific area associated with the brave? Somewhere that Mr. Howell might have visited and thought he saw the brave?" This was me, grasping at straws. Not pretty, I know.

"There is an area, not far from here, where many have reported seeing him. But he has appeared anywhere in a twenty-mile diameter around Santa Fe. It's possible your guest went on a hike or horseback riding and encountered his warning." He crossed his arms and let a few moments pass before continuing, "Are you wanting a guide to the local spot where the most people have reported seeing him?"

"I don't know how it will help me in this investigation, but it's worth a try." I felt a compulsion to find this spot, I couldn't explain it if I tried. "I was planning on setting a time to do this since I still have two more people to talk to this afternoon."

"I have some errands in town. I can pick you up on my way back, if that's better?"

I arranged to go with Miguel RunningElk later in the afternoon when Mason could go with me. I felt bad dragging him out after so little sleep, and another long day driving to take photos. But I knew he wouldn't want me going without him. I hoped I kept going on the few hours of sleep I had. I put some more eye drops in my eyes to soothe them more.

Carlos escorted Connor into the guest library, shut the door. He was wearing business casual and only a hint of aftershave floated by.

Connor stood and glared at me with his arms crossed. He had an attitude when the sheriff wasn't present.

"Sit down, Connor." I motioned with my hand to the chair.

"I'll stand. I don't plan on being here long." He smirked.

"I'd like to see you leave if Carlos feels I haven't finished." I smiled the sweetest smile I had. "But honest and quick answers to my questions will get you out of here." My smile vanished, and I gave him my mother's icy stare I was perfecting.

He remained standing, but his posture wasn't as cocksure. I accepted the challenge to hit him with some reality.

"I'm looking at how the ancient bow stolen from this very room was found in your suite, and how your colleagues think you are such a... what was the word? Slithering snake. That was the word; such a slithering snake you're their prime suspect. Which makes you mine, and likely the Sheriff's, too." I didn't think the Sheriff actually believed that, but Connor needed to see how it appeared.

"That's libelous and if you repeat that to anyone --" he pointed a finger at me, "I'll sue you so bad your grandchildren will be paying my estate." He smirked again.

I smiled my sweet smile again, "Oh, please do. The court trial will expose your lurid affair with Merritt's wife, oh my! Plus your various sabotage efforts to undermine Merritt, not to mention the aforementioned stolen bow-part of the murder weapon, found in your room. I wonder what that will do to your company and any future business? It won't be pretty."

"You wouldn't d-" He began.

I leaned forward to within an inch of his nose, "Try me." And then stood up straight again. "When you were being interrogated by the Sheriff, you threw Whittaker Tate under the bus. Well, I have spoken to Mr. Tate twice now and I'm not seeing it. And since he's not under arrest, I guess the Sheriff agrees with me. Question one: Besides executives, who at Howell

Venture would have an issue with both Merritt and Preston?" I stared at him, waiting for an answer.

He swallowed several times.

"Tick, tock Connor."

"Merritt was pretty merciless. I couldn't even begin to name all the fired or laid-off employees who might have it out for him, but Preston? That's a tough one. Unless Preston tried to save the company money by shafting people out of unemployment, severance, or other payments that I was unaware of. Merritt and Preston had little overlap when it came to employees." Once he started talking, he let his arms drop and placed his hands on his hips.

"Question two: Where were you last night at midnight? Don't say with Margaux or your wife, because that's too convenient."

"Well, I wasn't with Margaux, but there was a gal from the bar…" He had the barest decency to blush. "She's in room 326. I didn't leave her room until about 12:35 or so."

I shook my head but didn't comment on how he and his wife needed to divorce.

"Question three: Who do you think *might* set you up to take the fall for murder? I know that list is probably rather long, but try to limit it to the top three." I looked at my nails like they needed a manicure.

"You're not funny. I still think Tate is the most likely

to have murdered Merritt. I can only speculate and guess at reasons for his anger at Preston." He took a few breaths. "Oh, unless it had something to do with Preston not canceling the keyman insurance the company had out on him. I remember Tate visiting the company and reaming Preston out for still carrying the insurance on him, even though he wasn't employed by the company for months. But I was cool with Tate, I fought to keep him in charge." He had lost his bravado now.

I scoffed, "Yea, I bet you were altruistic."

We stood staring at each other.

"Hmm, keeping him insured as vital would be a slap in the face, I imagine." Keyman insurance, something I felt was an ethically and morally questionable act, where the company takes out insurance to be paid when a "key" employee dies to buffer any difficulty the business might experience. Just another way to make money on the employee, even in death it seemed to me. I can imagine that might be news that could set Whittaker Tate off in a rage since Merritt sabotaged and drove him out, yet they would still make money off him being so *valuable*.

Why hadn't Tate mentioned that? *Interesting.* I definitely needed to check Tate's alibi. But I wasn't done with Connor yet.

"So, how is it that Tate waltzed into the resort and

murdered not once, but twice? The second time in a hallway where anybody could have seen him. The first time was a stretch, but at least it was in the dark, in the garden among foliage for hiding. But walking the halls would be conspicuous with an arrow if not the bow, too. Hmmm, what do you think?" I really didn't know what I was doing. My fundamental premise was to keep asking questions from any angle and hope something was revealed that would help.

He rubbed a hand over his stubbly chin, "I guess the person would have to come in from a hiking trail out back to avoid the busiest spots. That's probably how he killed Merritt. I guess he was just lucky with Preston, slipped back out into the dark garden and made his way to the trails so nobody could have seen a car or anything."

Actually, that was a solid theory, and I kicked myself for not thinking of it. Even if it was somebody from the resort, they could slip out the back way, circle around and come in from the side and appear to join the crowd around the body later or just go to their room.

I thought of another question that I really wanted an answer to, and he was likely to know the answer. "Who is your staff informant?"

He crossed his arms again and seemed to puff up. "I don't know what you're talking about. Guests hear things when your employees don't think we're listening."

I almost laughed in his face, I probably should have. It was the other way around and I knew that from experience. I worked my way up through the hospitality industry ranks. Staff were invisible for the most part, unless a guest wanted to blame something on them.

"I don't believe you. Now, who has been telling you what I'm up to? You can tell me or I'll have to join your little conclave and start asking all of them."

He eventually gave up Emelio, the kid who handed me the note to meet somebody in the sauna. I would deal with him later.

A few more minutes of repetitive questions and I let Connor go. At least I uncovered Tate confronting Preston over the "key man" insurance. Still nothing on the wild idea that another employee might have a grudge, even with the cold-hearted management style.

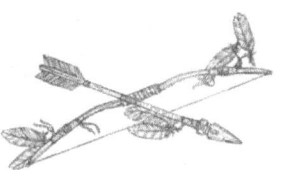

CHAPTER 12

*C*arlos returned with Margaux before I considered how I would approach my time with her. But then it wasn't like I had a grand plan for any of these sessions. It still surprised me these people agreed to talk to me.

"Mrs. Howell, please have a seat." I waved my hand to the chair, and she sat down.

"The last time we spoke, I neglected to give my condolences. I'm sorry for your loss." She nodded and sniffed. I waited a few heartbeats before continuing, "I was hoping to chat with you and see if you might have some insights into what has happened. You may not even realize you are aware of something significant." Apparently I was employing the *we need your help* approach.

"Did you know Preston Richards well?"

"I wouldn't say I knew him at all. I had met him a few times at office parties."

"I thought he was close with your husband until recently. He and his wife didn't come to your house for dinner or vice versa?" I asked in an even tone.

"I guess Merritt and Preston had a rather close working relationship, but they didn't spend time together outside of work." She sniffed again for effect. She wasn't an actress by any stretch of the imagination.

She just confirmed what Tate said about limited contact outside of the office.

So anything warranting murder involving them both must be work related.

"Here is where you might help me and the police. It seems highly likely the same person killed Preston who killed your husband. Can you think of anybody who has a grudge or hard feelings towards both of them?"

"I really wouldn't know. The police could find out if there were any lawsuits, I guess. Otherwise, I can only think of Whittaker Tate. I don't know how much Merritt involved Preston in taking over Tate's company, but it's possible." She seemed uninterested in the extent of her late husband's ruthless takeover actions. I would have found them shocking, personally.

"I have to ask, where were you last night from eleven-thirty to midnight?"

"Honey, I was in my room enjoying the liquor we

stocked. This healthy place doesn't have a decent bar or serve much in the way of alcohol. Merritt and I stocked up as soon as we got into town. I was alone, so don't bother asking. If I'd known I needed an alibi, I would have brought somebody to my room."

"I've been told that Merritt was rather a heartless leader. Were you aware of any angry employees who had a grudge against him that might include Preston?" I watched to see if she thought of anyone.

"Oh, you would have to be more specific. Sure, he wasn't liked much. But he felt that was to be expected. He never mentioned anybody dangerous that worried him." She appeared bored by the conversation.

"Considering what happened, it would seem he should have worried more about who he was ticking off." Her lackadaisical attitude towards his murder was getting to me, so I couldn't help myself when I added, "Gee, do you think the murderer might be mad at you as well? I mean, it's not like you were influencing him to be a better person?"

Her mouth fell open in a surprised "oh." Margaux shot out of the library once I said we were done. That was the end of my questioning the remaining suspects, but not the end of my day.

Carlos broke his silence after a few seconds alone, "They all pointed fingers at each other and didn't give us anything new to work with. I don't know what good that did."

"I agree. It seemed like a pointless task. But I learned that Whittaker Tate argued with Preston. That was a new piece of information." Which made Tate my prime suspect. I didn't want to point a finger at him after everything he had gone through, but he was definitely at the top of my list.

Carlos left me in the library and closed the door so I could think. I phoned Detective Sullivan and filled him in on my day and the revelation about Whittaker Tate. I mentioned the all-encompassing *disgruntled employee* notion to him too. While he thanked me for the information, he encouraged me to stop.

"Your employer can't expect anything more from you, and if you ask me, this was too much already."

I wouldn't bet on Chandler Carlton being satisfied yet since I hadn't fixed the situation.

"You wouldn't happen to know if Yates Aldrich's alibi of another poker game is valid? Or Whittaker Tate's claim he was with an investor in the bar at his hotel?" I crossed my fingers that he would actually tell me.

"We checked their alibis. I'll tell you so you don't go wasting everybody's time. They appear to be legitimate alibis for Preston's murder."

That just knocked Tate out as the prime suspect. It

left me with Connor or Margaux. I doubted Connor would have incriminated himself with the bow found in his room. So it would seem Margaux now took the number one slot. I had a difficult time seeing her using a bow and arrow to kill, she might break a nail. She was more the hire somebody type. That was completely up to the police to find a connection like that.

I stood up and stretched. I had to deal with the employee who was informing the Howell Venture group on my activities. I phoned Graciella and told her to bring Emilio to the offices. She was glad to round him up and deliver him. I had a feeling he would get an ear full from her, which made me smile.

I waited in Audrey's office and Graciella literally shoved him in the door and ranted in Spanish, shaking her finger at him. She left when Jonathon joined us.

Emilio's eyes were enormous, and he shifted in place.

Jonathan broke the heavy silence, "You have broken our trust in you, Emilio. Your job entails keeping private many things about our guests. But it also means you keep our procedures and details of our work behind the scenes to yourself. You have betrayed the trust we placed in you." Jonathan stared at him.

Emilio's eyes filled with tears, but he said nothing in his own defense. I was used to defensive, even hot headed employees when they were reprimanded. This kid was scared of losing his job, which made me feel bad.

"I looked over your record. You've had no other issues, you show up on time, and your reviews have shown you are a hard worker." He sighed, "I am at a loss to understand this."

Jonathan looked at me as if gaging my attitude in the situation.

I had absolutely no authority in this matter, but I think I understood Jonathan's silent plea and Emilio's heartache. "I wonder if, since he has a spotless record, Emilio might receive a written reprimand for his file and see if that resolves the issue?"

Emilio looked at me with surprise. Jonathan released a breath. Audrey closed her eyes.

"Emilio, if I were to just give you a written reprimand, do you promise to never let this happen again? You never share our business or a guest's information with anybody. Can you do that?"

A tear slid down his face, "I promise, sir. I will never do it again. I swear." His voice broke.

"Okay, the matter is settled. I will review your work in two weeks. You may go back to your duties now."

Emilio swallowed and left. I wouldn't be surprised if he spent a few minutes in the bathroom to pull himself together. He had almost lost his job, and from his reaction I suspected that his family needed the money.

I looked at my phone. It was nearing time to meet with Miguel RunningElk. I had a text message from Mason saying he saw my note and would meet me in the lobby. I had hit a wall and exhaustion was seeping through me. It was too late in the afternoon for coffee if I wanted to sleep tonight. I had to sleep tonight.

I took a break in the nearest bathroom and scrubbed my face with handfuls of cold water. It helped a little, but I knew I was running out of steam fast. My reflection in the mirror confirmed I looked as bad as I felt. *How can my hair look tired? That isn't fair.* I put more eyedrops in my red eyes to soothe them.

I made my way to the lobby and found Mason already in conversation with Mr. RunningElk. They were smiling and animated in their discussion. He showed only slight signs of little sleep around his eyes, otherwise he seemed fine. *Really not fair!*

"Hello babe. Miguel here was also a Marine. Small world, huh?" He smiled his full wattage grin.

"Oh, I was a few years before you. I think you got the softer, gentler Marine Corps. Not like in my day!" He laughed. "But to get down to business. We're driving a little way. It isn't far as the crow flies, but we have to take roads that aren't direct. I'll try to make the trip short so you two can get some rest this evening."

Mason lifted his backpack with his photography gear, "Would it be okay if I bring my camera and take some photographs?"

RunningElk considered for a few seconds, "Go ahead and bring your camera. I only ask that you follow my direction. If the spirits in this place don't like the camera, you honor that."

"Absolutely, I will follow your lead, no questions asked." Mason affirmed.

We piled into RunningElk's pickup that was covered in dirt from the unpaved roads he traveled. The seats were comfortable, and I was asleep with my head on Mason's shoulder before long.

A rough landscape with scrub brush and yucca fighting for survival in the rocky terrain surrounded me. I stood on a ledge. The rock wall supporting the ledge was layered with strips of light tan and dark reddish-brown sandstone with weather worn pockmarks and a cave opening. A light shined inside the cave and I felt drawn to explore. I cautiously stepped along the narrow ledge towards the cave entrance. I looked down at the two hundred foot drop and felt weak. The cave was before me; the light shifting like somebody was moving inside. I saw -

"Wake up Babe." Mason was shaking my shoulder, and I woke with a start.

For a few seconds, I was disoriented and looked around. "Sorry, I must've dozed off." I said to get my thoughts together. The dream was still in my mind, and

I realized with a jolt that we were parked exactly where my dream had started, only up high. I shook my head to clear the last cobwebs of the dream. *Could I still be dreaming?*

As soon as I stepped down from the truck and the afternoon heat hit me like a sledgehammer, I knew this wasn't a dream. We walked a few hundred yards down a path with hard packed dirt everywhere and startled lizards darting from the shade of rocks and plants. There were prickly pear cactus and yucca among the scrub brush scatter around.

RunningElk stopped and pointed up the sandstone rocky crag, "It was up there about eighty years ago where the bow and arrow were discovered."

I felt sweat run down my back, but a chill shot through me. I had just dreamt of this very place, only I was high up the side of the rocks. The only logical explanation was I must have seen a picture somewhere, and then my subconscious used it for a dream. That had to be it.

RunningElk continued, "The legend had been handed down verbally for a few generations about the young brave who delivered vengeance on the men who abducted our maidens. And for just as long, we've had people claim to have seen the brave. Whether you consider him a spirit or an illusion doesn't matter, because these people were not the loco type, they were rational and clear thinking." He spoke slowly, letting us absorb his words. "Then eighty years ago, a young man in our tribe was out hunting rabbits when he was led to that cave by a flickering light." He paused and pointed to a dark oblong up on the rock several hundred feet high. "Naturally, he climbed up. There were a few items in the cave, but the bow and arrows were wrapped in a red wool blanket in the back. They were in good condition, but we don't know why the legendary brave left the items in that cave. The archeology experts came, but found no evidence that a person had lived there." He was silent long enough to denote he was finished.

I waited as long as I could, "Do you know who this young brave was? Maybe a name or more about his life and death?"

"The same legend is told with Cochise or even Geranimo as the avenging man. I believe it is an otherwise insignificant young man who took two close friends, and like a Seal team rescued the three maidens. Because Cochise or Geranimo led bigger missions in a strategic war for their lands, not for three young maidens. This was a smaller, deeply personal attack for the woman he loved, but also for his small tribe's sake, so they weren't marked for annihilation as an easy target. I suspect that the tribe may have even moved away or became more reclusive for survival." He spoke matter-of-factly about such a moving tale.

Since I had fallen asleep on the drive, I wasn't sure where we were. "How far is the resort from here?"

"As I mentioned, it isn't far. We are actually three-quarters of a mile northwest from Enchanted Canyon Resort if you walked directly that way." He pointed to the right, along the rocky wall's path.

I wondered if the back trail at the resort could lead this direction. "Do you think I could hike from there easily?"

"Oh yes, I've done it. Not difficult at all. If you know the trail, you can get here pretty quickly."

I would have to find out. Tomorrow.

Mason had been quietly studying our surroundings until now, "Why do you think this brave's spirit will appear to Julienne?"

They must have chatted while I slept.

"I sense his presence, his thirst for justice is strong around her. She has his determination to see the guilty answer for their crimes. He will be drawn to her." He gazed directly into my eyes and I became self-conscious and looked away.

As we were trudging back to the truck, I heard a scuffle on the hard packed dirt behind me and turned.

There he was. The Native American brave dressed in simple buckskin pants and a matching loose fitting top with some beadwork stitched on the shoulders. His thick black hair in side braids tied with leather strips and what I suspected was an eagle and an owl feather dangling. He looked me in the eye and for a few moments I felt his strength of will surge through me. In my mind *the guilty must pay for their deeds* boomed, as if he had pounded them into my head. His image wavered like a water reflection being stirred, and he disappeared.

"Julie, what's wrong?" Mason called.

"Nothing, I thought I heard something." I turned toward the truck, shook my head, and tried to discount what I had just seen. My lack of sleep and Running-Elk's story had taken hold in my imagination. That was all.

During the drive back, I was silent. The weird dream I had and whatever I saw plagued my mind. It had to be my lack of sleep getting to me. Tonight I had to get a solid eight hours or more of sleep. No excuses.

Mr. RunningElk dropped us off at the door and assured me I could call him anytime with questions. We walked into the resort and came face-to-face with Tiffany, who had clearly been waiting for Mason's return.

I really wasn't in the mood, but I also feared if I said anything with my lack of sleep I would regret the scene that could develop in front of the employees.

At least she wasn't dressed like a night at the opera. She wore a simple sky-blue sundress and canvass shoes that were appropriate for the weather and environment.

Mason let out a weary sigh, "Tiffany, I have nothing to say to you. It's pretty clear you came here thinking you could break us up. That's never going to happen, no matter how hard you try."

"Actually, I would like to talk to Julienne please. Privately." She looked directly at me without malice. She wasn't friendly and sunshine, but she wasn't hostile either.

My eyebrows reached for the sky. Was my sluggish mind playing tricks on me? Did she actually ask nicely to talk with me? I nearly turned and left, but that wouldn't solve anything. I might as well hear what she had to say.

Mason looked at me with surprise evident in his eyes and a soupçon of worry.

"I'll be up in a few moments. Don't worry." I told Mason and gave him a kiss on the cheek.

"Would you join me for a friendly drink?" Tiffany even managed a slight smile. Her perfume enveloped me, Hot and Sexy from that upscale lingerie chain.

"I could use a little drink after the day I've had." I said by way of warning her I was liable to unleash a verbal thrashing if she pushed me, especially if the drink was spiked.

We were seated at the restaurant at a table for two in an isolated corner of the room. I didn't have to fear being overheard unless we started yelling. Normally I wouldn't worry about that, but I sensed she could push my buttons and I would be compelled to raise my voice in a most unprofessional manner.

I ordered the mock Paloma. It was quickly becoming a favorite with its refreshing citrus flavor of grapefruit although I really would've liked a splash of Tequila added. I planned on learning to make them at home. Tiffany ordered a cranberry and ginger ale concoction.

The silence stretched out and became uncomfortable. After the server brought our drinks, I got this flimsy detente moving.

"I wish they served cocktails rather than mocktails." My sad attempt at breaking the ice.

"Yes, I could use a glass of wine." She twisted her napkin around a finger.

I took a big swallow of my drink, and cleared my throat, "So, you wanted to talk to me?" I never claimed to be a scintillating conversationalist.

"Right. I don't know if you have met Mason's family?" She scrutinized her glass.

I hadn't expected this topic. "I've met a few of his

family. Mostly his sister. I had what I can only call a run-in with his father a few months ago."

She let out a sigh, "That would explain why he tracked me down."

My mouth fell open. Mason's father had found an old girlfriend of Mason's to break us up. I knew we weren't ever likely to be close, but that was harsh. I snapped my mouth shut.

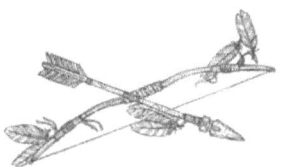

CHAPTER 13

"He sought you out? For what?" I had a pretty good guess it had something to do with her coincidental stay here.

"He convinced me you were trying to entrap Mason into marrying you for the status." She had the decency to look away and her face reddened.

I took a few minutes to filter the first comments that sprang up and waited for a calm reply to enter my head. "So I supposedly wanted Mason's status of hanging out with celebrities? Actually, I broke up with him over his undercover bodyguard work with celebrities. And furthermore, Mason's father doesn't even know me." I took a breath to continue when she interrupted me.

"No, the general's celebrity." She said.

"Wait, *his* celebrity... as a general?" I shook my

head like I was trying to get an annoying buzz in my ear to stop.

"Yes. He's an important man, and he's considering a political career. So, yes, he thought you wanted into the family for the status he has now and will garner in the future." She looked me directly in the eyes now.

"I can appreciate that he's achieved a high rank, but I grew up around the military. I've good friends who were children of officers, and even a two-star general's daughter who attended my sleepovers. It's not a big deal to me, it never has been. Actually, Mason was afraid for me to meet his father because he's so caustic. Maybe the general ought to think of how ashamed his children are of him because of his behavior." Yep, I probably shouldn't have said some of that.

Tiffany stared at me with a blank look. "Mason's ashamed of the general? But, he's important, people look up to him."

"So? How he treats his family is more of a testament to his true character. I'm not impressed, at all." Her other comments hit me, "And who said anything about marriage at this point?" I took a deep breath and motioned with my hand for her to continue. "And you went along with it?"

"I... Yes, I went along with it. For Mason's sake, of course." She said. Her attempt at an innocent and beneficent look failed. Yep, there was something in this for her.

"And Mason's father being General Sheridan means nothing to you? Because you certainly seem swayed by his *status*." I smirked.

"I was just helping, for Mason's sake. That's all." She made innocent doe eyes.

"Why are you telling me all this now? You could've just left." Which I would have preferred.

"I wanted to make amends." She said it without sarcasm or choking.

I didn't believe her at all. But I couldn't understand why she would try to make nice now.

I stood up, "If that's all, I've had an exceptionally long day, and I really don't care to spend any more of it in this conversation. Goodnight and goodbye." I turned and walked out.

I was getting angrier with each step, though. Mason's father was really a piece of work. No wonder Mason hadn't wanted me to meet the man. I wasn't sure how Mason would react to the news. When I entered our room, he spun around and came to me. I suspect he had been pacing.

"What did Tif want?" He blurted out. I couldn't blame his lack of greeting since he had to be as exhausted as I was.

"Well, I'm not sure of her ulterior motive. She

claims your father convinced her I was only seeking status dating his son and enlisted her to save you from my wicked clutches." I didn't soften the impact or phrase it nicely. "Oh, and she wants to make amends." I tossed that last part out to see if he felt the same as I did on that score.

He blew out a breath, "Ha! My father wouldn't need to convince her, just tell her what he wanted done. She was always trying to impress my father above all else. As for making amends, I hope you saw through that ploy." He ran a hand through his unruly locks, making a curly strand fall over an eye.

"Oh, I left at that point, after I said too much in my frustration. It slipped out that the general should be concerned with his children being ashamed of him." I held my breath. Would he be upset I let that out?

The edges of his lips gradually quirked, up and he shook his head, "I doubt Tif would ever tell him that, but I should've years ago." He held his arms out, and I stepped into them.

There was a knock at the door, and I cursed under my breath. I was enjoying the hug.

"I ordered some room service since neither of us have had dinner. That should be it now."

Once he mentioned food, I realized I was famished. I really wanted less healthy cuisine like a Chili Rellenos or Tamales. I would have to settle for whatever healthy option Mason ordered, because I just wanted to eat and then get a decent night's sleep. My hopes of reading through the rest of Beverly's research would probably have to wait until morning. I wasn't sure I would stay awake through dinner.

Mason opened the door, "What're you doing here?"

"Hello to you, too. Are you going to make me stay in the hall?" A woman's voice said. It wasn't Tiffany, though.

Mason stepped aside and his sister, Marisa, strode in with rolling luggage.

I met her halfway and gave her a big hug that she returned.

"Now that's a proper welcome. Did you see that brother, she seems happier to see me than my own flesh and blood." She smiled to soften the words. "By the way, you're looking ragged around the edges." She winked at me, "Is she wearing you out?"

Mason covered his face with a hand, "Sis, we got about two hours of sleep last night after somebody left a dead body at our door. That's probably why I'm not as welcoming." He gave her a bear hug.

"As excuses go, that's a good one." She looked between us. "You can fill me in on the dead body later. Even though it's hard to put off hearing that one. But, I came as damage control as soon as I found out Dad sent Tiffany here to sabotage you two. She hasn't caused tension between you, has she?" Her eyes flashed a stormy warning, and I wouldn't want to be Tiffany at the moment.

Mason looked at me, "Now we know why she claimed to want to make amends! I would back pedal if Marisa was on the warpath after me, too."

"She tried, but Mason was onto her schemes from the beginning and kept shutting her down." I told her.

"Although, she told Julie that Dad sent her." Mason stared into Marisa's eyes.

Marisa groaned, "I'm sorry. Look, I won't take up any more of your time. I wanted to give the desk some time to arrange my room. I stopped and ate so I just want to go to sleep since Tiffany can wait until tomorrow." She stood up to go, "I won't be in your hair much, I just want to run interference with Tiffany, and then I'll leave you two alone."

We hugged goodnight and when she opened the door, our room service was just wheeling up our dinner.

I had the grilled salmon fillet with cauliflower mash that was a low carb substitute for mashed potatoes. It was superb, or I was famished because it seemed like the most delicious meal in my life. Mason similarly devoured his herb-marinated chicken with roasted sweet potato.

I tried to read Beverly's research, but a full stomach and lack of sleep left me unable to focus on the words. Mason was already passed out and I couldn't fight it. I drifted away with the laptop in my lap.

When I woke up, Mason was gone on another photography shoot. He left a note with apologies over his father and Tiffany, tender sentiments, and excitement that he might get the lightning storm over the desert today. He was getting a lot of great photos that he would spend the next few weeks making even better with post processing in Photoshop.

I knew he was far more upset over his father's attempt to break us up than he would ever admit, and this was only making their relationship more fraught. I wish there were something I could do, but it seemed I had done enough when I spoke up to the general a few months back. That meeting hadn't gone well, and I was partly to blame for not biting my tongue, but I didn't care if the man was his father and a general, I couldn't sit by while he berated Mason.

I settled down to read Beverly's research, flipping through the attached files in the email she sent me. She sent what interesting notices were published. One file was about key man insurance, and Howell Venture was mentioned. I would save that to read later. There were articles where various employees were referenced. It might contain a tidbit that could help, but that would have to wait till later, too. I was just wading into a business magazine's lengthy write up about Howell Venture when my room phone rang.

"Oh good, you're up. I hoped I wasn't disturbing you if you slept in." Marisa's chipper voice sang out. "I found out through the grapevine about the body dumped at your door. I thought you could use a spa treatment. My treat."

"That is so generous of you. But I should get to work. Training has been sporadic because of questioning guests about the murder." I didn't want to offend Marisa.

"Well, I took the liberty of talking with Audrey, and she said you deserve the break. Just check in with them once you're done with your treatment. How does eight this morning sound for the spa?"

And just like that, I was booked for a spa treatment in thirty minutes. I grew up an only child, but I was feeling like I had a big sister looking after me. It was an odd feeling, comforting yet a little intrusive. Just like what my friends all said about their siblings.

I closed down my laptop and promised I would at least skim over all that research… soon. I scrambled out the door and walked over to the adjoining spa complex. It was eighty thousand square feet with more than just the spa. It included cardio and weight rooms, dance and yoga studios, the pilates studio where we had the press conference, indoor cycling gym, racquetball, wallyball, squash courts, steam rooms, whirlpools, and private sun decks. I hadn't had the chance to explore the facility, so I took a few minutes to look around quickly and made it to the spa on time.

I selected the fifty-minute signature massage and was led into a private room with soft lighting and gentle Native American flute music playing. At first my mind churned over all the aspects of the two murders. I was down to four suspects unless I opened up the possibilities to disgruntled employees.

Merritt and Preston had very little in common outside of the business, so the motive had to be Howell Venture related. I didn't like Connor, but I didn't think he suddenly hid the stolen legendary bow under his hotel bed without realizing the maid service would find it. Margaux had plenty of motive when it came to her husband, but none with Preston. Yates Aldrich was a disreputable competitor of Merritt's, but appeared to have nothing that would tie him to Preston. That brought me Whittaker Tate who probably still blamed Merritt for his wife's suicide on top of ousting him from his own company, and Preston for keeping a key man insurance policy on him. Talk about adding insult to injury! Yates tossing out regular employees was a long shot in my mind, but I didn't want to just dismiss the idea and miss something. Not that I could look up every dismissed employee. I worried the executives were close to checking out, and that made it more difficult for the police, too.

After a few minutes, I relaxed and dozed. My mind still acknowledged sounds and movement, but I was detached. Eventually I realized my attendant had finished the massage and left. Did I fall asleep and she didn't want to interrupt me? I was warm and relaxed, so just opening my eyes was a fight. I glanced around; I was alone and according to the clock it was only a few minutes after when the massage should have ended.

I sat up on the table and a slip of paper that had rested on my chest drifted to my lap. I opened the single fold to find a few words scrawled in rough print, as if a person used their non-dominant hand to write it. MIND YOUR OWN BUSINESS AND YOU WON'T GET HURT.

A chill went down my back and my heart leapt into overdrive. I hadn't even noticed this placed on me. The killer had been in this room alone with me, and I had sensed nothing. My hand holding the note shook. I busied myself with getting up; I wanted out of the spa. My massage therapist entered as I was standing and attempting to keep my legs from shaking.

"I was about to check on you, you had fallen asleep. I'm sure you needed it. Is there anything else I can help you with? Perhaps a nice mud cocoon wrap?" She asked without a hint of evasion or deception.

"No, thank you. I thought I heard somebody enter the room after you left. Did you see anybody?"

"No ma'am, I didn't see anybody come near this room."

"I really need to get back to work. This was a perfect rejuvenating break. Thank you." I slipped her a tip I had brought with me and nearly ran to the locker room. Within minutes I was back in the main hotel's breakfast grill. I hadn't eaten yet, and I always think better on a full stomach. I had settled on an egg frittata with spinach and broccoli and breakfast potatoes. No coffee. I opted for hot herbal tea.

I debated taking the note to the police. According to Detective Sullivan, the bow and arrow recovered contained no fingerprints or other evidence, so I suspected that note didn't have any either. Plus, I didn't want to hear the commands to stop working on this. I would just have to change tactics and cover my backside.

As I ate, I thought about the note, now in a pocket. The person doesn't want to hurt me, or I'd have had something unpleasant happen. First being locked in the sauna, and now this threatening note. Both times were scare tactics, and nothing that could harm me. But I couldn't count on that remaining the case.

Graciella hadn't called. I had a few questions and perhaps she could help me get some answers. I needed to visit Detective Sullivan, and I hoped he would share what he had learned, although he had every right to keep information to himself.

Marisa walked into the restaurant and joined me. She was always the fashion plate with a terra cotta peasant blouse with designer jeans and knee high velvet boots. She had a simple turquoise necklace with a matching bracelet and earrings.

"You always look so put together. I feel like a dumpy mess compared to you."

"Oh, stop. You have that effortless beauty that makes everything your wear look classic." She smiled.

I nearly choked on my tea. I think she was actually serious, too.

"Thank you so much for the massage, it was divine." It wasn't her fault a killer snuck in and ruined the moment. It had been incredibly kind of her.

"I'm so glad you took advantage of it." She waved a server over and asked for the healthy Tofu scramble. Then she sat back in her chair and looked at me, "By-the-by, Tiffany checked out this morning. We had a brief chat before she left. If she even sniffs in your direction, please let me know."

This time I nearly choked on a bite of breakfast potatoes. "Did you threaten her?" My voice was a whisper.

"Let's just say that I know a few juicy details from her time dating Mason that she wouldn't want out on Facebook, Twitter, and any alumni news, let alone a phone call to her parents. I can't stand manipulative little wenches."

I was very grateful that Marisa and I got along well, because this side of her wasn't one I wanted to experience.

"I feel I should apologize for my father. He has no excuse for his actions." She didn't look me in the eye.

"He is the only one who can apologize for his actions. I appreciate the gesture, though. He is losing his son, perhaps irreparably with his attitude and behavior." I let out a heavy sigh.

"I'll attempt to get that through his thick skull when I see him next. I want my family to get closer, not torn apart. Thank you for not letting this impact your relationship with Mason." She smiled, "You're good for him, and I want you two to have a shot at long term." She raised her hands, "However that looks for you two."

Her healthy tofu scramble arrived, and we chatted about her starting a new job in a critical care unit. She's a nurse that specialized in acute care. She was excited, and yet apprehensive about starting over in a new job.

I looked at my watch and excused myself to report

to Audrey about work today. We hugged before I left. She was the closest to a sister I've ever come.

I reported to Audrey my four interviews yesterday, and what I would like to do today. I wanted to do more training with the front desk people, even if I caught only one or two of the young women I had begun training depending on their schedules. I shared how I wanted to go into town to talk to Detective Sullivan and also follow up with some questions for Graciella. She was happy with that, so I went directly to the front desk.

Maria was on duty, but she was only working a few hours. I put everything else out of my mind and began showing her a few advanced features for looking at a client's history from reservation dates to room prefer-ences, cancellations to extra charges. I answered her questions from the brief lesson we had before. After two hours that sped past, she was picking the training up well. It was the end of Maria's shift, and I promised to check in tomorrow to answer questions and review.

I checked back with Audrey because I had an idea. "Maria is picking up the training fairly easily. I'm just grateful our software is similar to your existing system. Are there questions on the management side?"

I went over a few advanced features to answer her questions for the executive side of the software with financial statements.

"Before I go, I had another thought. I When Merritt was killed, did the police find anything in the foliage or landscaping? Were you the point person they talked to?" I asked.

"I don't know what they found, if anything. Carlos handled everything with the police once he arrived. Why?"

"I'm running out of ideas to follow and feel like I should start at the beginning. I'd like to look over the area with Carlos, if that's possible."

She picked up her office phone and called Carlos, "Can you spare a few minutes to show Julienne the… um… spot where Mr. Howell died, and share anything the police had found?" She hung up. "Carlos will meet you out there in just a few minutes."

CHAPTER 14

I wasn't sure this would have any results, but I was running out of ideas. I needed an epiphany. The only person who seemed to have a motive regarding both Merritt and Preston was Whittaker Tate. But he supposedly had an alibi for the time of Preston's murder at his hotel meeting with an investor. Could that alibi be a lie? What about the old bow being found in Connor's room? Could Connor and Margaux have killed them both as a team? What if Preston knew something that pointed to Merritt's killer and I was wasting time looking for a personal motive when it was to shut him up? Then there was Yates Aldrich. I wouldn't put it past him to sneak into the lodge and kill them both. Or worse, what if there were two killers and the two deaths weren't related at all?

Carlos walked up and broke my mental wrestling.

"I understand you want to go over that night." He led the way to a section that had some orange cones blocking off use. "They finished all the forensic evidence collection, but I wanted to keep from encouraging the morbidly curious from trampling the vegetation with the cones."

I turned to him, "I'm grasping at straws now. Did the police find any forensic tidbits? Anything?"

He nodded, "It isn't much, but there are some footprints off the sidewalk among the flowering brush, right about where they estimate the killer struck him. They think he crawled a short way. I'll show you."

I followed him into the landscaped foliage alongside the sidewalk with palm trees just over head. He was careful to show me where to stand and pointed. I could just make out some slight footsteps.

"Looks like a hiking boot to me, but small." I said.

"That's what the Detective said. He didn't know if they could find a match in their databases." Carlos sighed.

"Did they follow to see where the prints go?"

"Yes, apparently the footprints stop at the hiking trails to the back. The ground was too hard packed from there on for any impressions that night."

"Hmmm. Did they ask housekeeping to be looking for a hiking boot with that tread?" I asked.

"I don't know about that. Maybe the detective

asked when the bow was found in Connor's room?" He seemed skeptical.

"Well, looks like later this afternoon I may have to take a hike and see what I can find."

"I don't know, miss. Maybe you should wait for your boyfriend to go with you?"

That settled my mind. Mason was showing how tired he really was with getting up before sunrise to do his photography and then my running him ragged with investigating in the evenings. I would do the hike by myself, with a compass, my cell phone, and pepper spray on hand. I didn't need a bodyguard everywhere I went.

Besides, the chances of my actually finding anything were slim to none. I know the killer was trying to scare me away, but taking a hike on a trail is innocent and part of the activities offered, so it isn't really investigating. Still, I would ask for a map of the hiking trail, and make it clear I'm just hiking for enjoyment. Nobody needed to know I was keeping my eyes open for the escape route of Merritt's killer.

I took out my cell phone and snapped a photo of the boot print, working the angle to get good detail of the tread. I thanked Carlos and returned to my room, where I felt comfortable calling Graciella. The note must have gotten to me more than I wanted to admit. If I was going to downplay my hike as just recreation and not looking for where the killer went, then I needed to do as much in private as possible.

I wondered about the boot prints. If they were truly the killer's prints, they seemed rather small. Smaller than my shoe size. I thought of Margaux, but I didn't know what size hiking boots she wore. Although, I thought she wore a larger size than I. I couldn't recall any of the men (Connor, Whittaker, or Yates) having smallish feet. Not that I was paying attention to their feet.

Plus, what did the prints left by the back hiking trails mean? Did that suggest the killer wasn't staying at the resort, or did it simply mean they escaped that direction and possibly came back through the front for appearance's sake? I thrust the swirling thoughts aside and called Graciella.

"Yes." She answered.

"It's me, Julienne. I'm gathering it's been quiet since I haven't heard from you?"

"I think once the Howell group got wind of all of us listening to them for any information, they shut their gossipy mouths. You can blame Emilio for that, I sure do."

"I was wondering if Detective Sullivan had asked you to keep an eye out for a pair of small hiking boots, as you do your daily housekeeping of rooms?"

"No, he didn't. Should I be? It's getting close to

being a moot point. Several of the Howell people will leave tomorrow afternoon. Unless the detective instructed them to stay longer."

"Does Margaux Howell have any hiking boots? Do you recall any in her suite?" I asked, still grasping at straws. I didn't want to think of the killer leaving and the difficulty to solve it with everyone dispersed.

Graciella chuckled in a guttural sound full of derision. "That woman wouldn't go hiking, she might run into wildlife of any sort, besides she might break a sweat. But no, she only has heels of varying heights, nothing so practical as a hiking boot."

Well crap.

"How about Emilio? Has he been attentive to anyone of the Howell group?" I was considering if the killer had asked him to slip me the note to meet in the sauna back when I was locked in.

"Oh, Emilio has worked here a few years and some returning guests recognize him, and he makes them feel pampered. But I don't know of one guest being close to him. Sorry."

"Did any employees see a person enter Connor's room before you found the bow? Anybody that wasn't Connor or his wife?"

"I will ask around, but I don't think so. They would have said something by now."

I let out a sigh and asked her to keep her ears open for me, then I said goodbye.

I went to the plaza in downtown Santa Fe for lunch and braved the oppressive heat to find a little restaurant that was packed. Fortunately, their air conditioning was working. I wanted some authentic food, so I got the Calabacitas Quesadilla with roasted squash, corn, chopped green chile, onions, tomatoes, chicken, and cheese in two flour tortillas and a side of green chile fries. The fries smothered in green chili probably weren't old world authentic, but I had to try them. It was heaven. My lunch spot was nowhere near the police station. After lunch I made my way from the city square southwest on Cerrillos Road a few miles to the station house. I had borrowed the resort car and found the air conditioner struggled to cool the interior.

The station was across from a mall and looked like an office complex they had taken over. Once inside, the regular sense of disillusionment with humanity hung heavy with the aroma of dirtier and sweatier citizens. As lovely as Santa Fe is, it has its criminal element and people struggling through life like everywhere else. I asked to see Detective Sullivan and had to wait in a hard plastic chair in a lovely shade of puke green. This wasn't the sightseeing I had intended in my desire to see the world via working at resorts, but it was an education. I got a crash course in what opioid addiction looked like and what a "working girl" really dressed like. I stuck out in my turquoise blazer and matching slacks with tan pumps like a nun at a male strip club.

When the desk sergeant pointed the way to Detective Sullivan and declared he could see me now, I nearly ran. I skidded to a stop at his slightly battered desk and waited for him to acknowledge me.

He finally glanced up, then groaned and leaned back in his chair until I thought it would flip. "This is a first, you've made a special trip to see me." He looked me over in an efficient analytical way, "No sign of you're being mugged or accosted. So, why are you here?" He snapped his fingers, "You've finished all your little interviews with your list of suspects and now you want to see what cards I'm holding." He crossed his arms against his chest and leaned back even further until the chair squealed for mercy.

"There is no need to be snippy. Do you have a little spy working at the resort?" I lifted an eyebrow, attempting to lend an air of gravitas to my presence. After Emilio, I felt as though nothing was private at Enchantment Canyon Resort.

"I'm the professional here. I don't need spies or informants as long as citizens share what they know. I call Carlos and he tells me what is happening, like he should." He leaned forward, and the chair came crashing down onto its front legs. "He tells me you're doing your best and that you're forced by the resort owner to conduct your little show. So, I've been far more lenient than I should, but don't start wasting my time."

I plopped into his upholstered chair that was just as hard as a stone park bench despite the illusion of padding.

"Good, I don't need to beat around the bush or sweet talk you. I looked over Merritt's crime scene since that night isn't clear after his hand grabbed my ankle. I saw the bootprints leading to the hiking trails behind the resort. The boot prints and the bow and arrows left behind are the only evidence to go on?" I left it as a question, but he didn't reply.

I leaned back this time and crossed my arms, "Want to know what doesn't make sense to me? How is it that an old arrow that is at least eight decades or more old was shot from an equally old handmade bow andgot enough velocity to make it through the rib cage? Unless the shooter was so precise as to be suspicious in itself. That's been bothering me." Actually, I had just thought about it as I waited to see him.

He gave me a stoney glare in reply.

I continued talking, undeterred. "I've asked house-keeping to be-on-the-lookout for hiking boots that match that tread. I know it appears the murderer left after killing Merritt, which leads one to believe the killer wasn't staying at the resort. But I'm not so sure after Preston's murder." I stared into his eyes, regarding me with calculation. I swallowed a few times, suddenly suffering from a dry mouth.

"I'll share this with you because you won't leave this alone and you need to understand the level of skill this killer exhibits. The old bow and arrow weren't used, they were just props. Both Merritt and Preston had microscopic carbon and aluminum traces, and the entry wounds are consistent with a modern arrow with broadhead arrow point, typically used with a compound bow for game hunting. Not only was top of the line bow-hunting equipment used, but the kill shot for both of them was precisely between the ribs to hit the heart instantly. This is an extremely skilled killer, and you are no match for him." He grimaced at me as if he could intimidate me like a little girl. Although he was rather imposing, I'd give him that.

The modern bow and arrow was news to me. In light of the threatening note left for me after my massage, and being locked in the sauna, I wondered why this killer hadn't hurt me and really stopped me from investigating. It's hard to think of a killer having a line he won't cross, but what if it was a score to settle with Merritt and Preston and he or she didn't want to hurt me?

"You said 'no match for *him*,' do you think it's a

man?" I had a hard time envisioning Margaux ruining her manicure to become an expert at shooting a powerful bow. But I had no problem seeing Connor, Whittaker, or Yates using a bow in some macho mindset.

"Don't put words in my mouth." He started shuffling papers on his desk, a hint he was done with our chat.

"I wanted to run something by you that Yates Aldrich said to me. Although he keeps implicating Whittaker Tate, he also said there were many employees who had suffered from Merritt's policies when he took over the company. He felt any number of such employees could be behind the murders and even extend their grudge to Preston. Is that something you have been looking into?" I tried to keep my voice nonchalant, as if I found it only mildly interesting. Which wasn't hard. Mostly, I wanted to keep him talking.

"Miss LaMere, we have been looking into every solid lead, but Preston had been the most promising suspect until he was killed. I ruled out suicide in his case. A murder suicide would've tied the case up neatly, but he was definitely murdered. Now I really need to get back to work." He looked up from his paperwork, "Do us all a favor and tell your boss you've done everything you can and it's now in our hands."

"Mr. Tate had an argument with Preston Richards a few months ago. I uncovered that during my *little interviews* with my suspects." I said, hoping to keep him talking.

Although he didn't look up, he stopped shuffling papers for a split second. Then he took a hand and shooed me out.

Aha, so I had been thinking along the same lines as Detective Sullivan, thinking Preston was the most likely to have killed Merritt. My walk out of the station was by autopilot as I contemplated the conversation. I felt somewhat validated I'd been on track with my suspicions. I hadn't mentioned my sense of urgency to get some resolution to the murders before all the suspects packed up and went home, and any evidence would go with them. This wasn't good for the Resort. My mind kept churning over the murders as I drove back to the Resort.

I could be correct, and Whitaker Tate was the killer. He had plenty of motive with Merritt pushing him out of the company, destroying his life, and Preston continuing to have a Key Man Insurance policy on him to benefit the company that devastated him. Although that was what they called circumstantial evidence. Unless they found physical evidence, it was a slim chance he would be tried and imprisoned. I just wasn't convinced. He supposedly had alibis for the two murders. Those alibis were probably the only reason he was walking around free.

The road out of town to the resort wasn't busy as I mulled over what I had so far. I was frustrated. I was missing something and I could feel it. The Detective's warning kept repeating in my head, *this is a skilled killer and you are no match for him.* I knew I wasn't and didn't plan on going "head-to-head" with a double murderer. Unfortunately, I couldn't stop thinking about it. What were my chances of actually solving the case, really? But what matters is what the killer thinks I can uncover.

I got back to Enchanted Canyon as Blair was parking an older model Volvo that appeared to have seen better days. The silver paint was dull and oxidized and a few dings showed. It seemed things might not have gone so well for her since her husband died. She never mentioned her working, just that her husband had worked, and she cared for him through his illness. My heart went out to her.

We walked into the cool lobby from the hot exterior together and I noticed she had a bag from a department store.

"Got some shopping done, I see. Maybe a new outfit for your date?" I tried to keep a light, teasing voice to make her smile.

She looked at me and beamed like a teenager, "Oh,

I really shouldn't have splurged. Off the rack was the best I could do. Do you think he'll notice?"

"I don't think he'll notice at all if you smile like that at him." I meant it. She transformed when she smiled, her eyes that usually looked sad and tired glowed and she seemed ten years younger.

"Oh, go on." She blushed.

"I mean it, Blair. Enjoy the attention, you deserve it. Are you having a spa treatment?"

"I decided I would have them cut and style my hair for tonight. I should probably have my nails done, they are atrocious." She looked at her nails, they were short and a little ragged and calluses showed on a few fingers. "Can you believe how nervous I am?" She giggled as she scurried off to the elevator.

I hoped Blair and Whittaker found a new start. They both seemed to have had some rough times and this might be an excellent match, if he wasn't the killer. Gee, when did I get so sentimental? But I wanted to see her happy. She was a new person after the aura of depression and grieving lifted a little.

I went to my room and changed into something more suitable for a casual hike. Attempting to look like I was solely taking advantage of a resort amenity, I was careful what I wore. I dressed in jeans and a summer top with athletic shoes. I put my hair in a ponytail and grabbed a visor for the sun along with sunglasses and checked my image in the mirror. A tourist looked back, not a snoop looking for clues to a murderer. I slipped my compass in a pocket, my cell phone in a back pocket, and my portable pepper spray in the other front pocket. A bottle of water completed my accessories. I left a note for Mason just in case I was delayed.

I made a point of stopping at the front desk and talking to the gal about what sites to look for on the trail and got a printed map of the trail.

"We suggest you use some binoculars to enjoy the vistas." She informed me.

So I took a pair of lightweight binoculars they offered and hung them around my neck. The one thing I didn't prepare for was the blast furnace of heat that socked me the instant I stepped outside. It was a scorcher today, and I immediately sweat in every crevice. Oh, this was going to be hot climbing around on the hiking trail, I hoped it was as easy a trail as the map claimed. For a quick second I considered finding an umbrella to use, but that would only make any tricky climbing more difficult.

The trail started out at a bit of an angle upwards, taking me around a rock outcropping and out of sight from the resort. I stopped to consider this in the dark of night with the nearly full moon, as it was when Merritt was shot. It hadn't been strenuous or even rough on the trail thus far, and if a person were familiar with the path, I suppose it wouldn't have been difficult at all. Which made me consider how you shot a bow to kill in the moonlight. I crept slowly back on the trail until the resort was just in sight. The vantage point was elevated a good twenty feet and looked down at the resort. I located where Merritt was found.

I didn't expect it to be a clear shot, but it was. If the shooter was experienced at hunting big game with archery, I suppose the distance might have been a challenge but not impossible. I didn't know that for sure and made a mental note to research the accuracy of an arrow at that distance.

I turned and continued walking along the trail, my binoculars bouncing around my neck. If the shooter had been up here for the kill shot, what would be the next move? Well, the killer had to go down into the resort grounds and place the legendary old arrow in the wound without being seen. Dark-colored clothing would have helped with that.

I flashed back to Merritt holding onto my ankle and saying, *It's the curse... the curse got me!* If somebody wearing dark clothes appeared after an arrow shot you and they had dark makeup on their face to further go unnoticed, that would seem like a vision of the Native American brave from the legend. Okay, so not only was the killer likely wearing dark clothes, but potentially a darkened face.

After placing the ancient arrow in the wound, I shivered at the very thought, what would the killer do next? The longer he stayed on the resort grounds, the more likely he was to be seen and attempting to make it to a room would be near impossible without being spotted. Even circling around to the well lit parking lot was highly risky. This trail was the logical escape. So I continued on.

I wasn't sure what I was looking for, so I kept my eyes searching for anything out of place or maybe a good place to change clothes and hide a bow and arrow set. Another five minutes and I was drenched in sweat. I stopped to drink from my bottled water and swiped my forehead with my arm. I wasn't sure how long I could stay out in this brutal heat before I got heat stroke.

I found a scraggly tree tenaciously growing on the side of the hill and took refuge in its meager shadow. I watched as a rattlesnake slithered across the path I just walked. Once it was long gone, I breathed again.

I was reluctant to leave the shade of the lone tree. I took my binoculars and searched the surrounding area, particularly further along the trail and up above my position. It was just yesterday evening that I was somewhere out there with Mason and Miguel RunningElk. I was positive this was the same rocky hill Miguel said the cave where the Vengeful Brave's bow and arrow were found.

I stared at the trail ahead and swore I saw the boot prints on the trail ahead, stark and obvious, even shimmering. I shook my head and looked again. They were gone. *The heat must be getting to me.*

CHAPTER 15

*W*hile I stood in the shelter of the tree's shadow, dark clouds swept in. Within a mere five minutes, the sun was now blocked, and the skies grew increasingly dark. Promising I would return early tomorrow before it got so hot, I started back to the resort. I had made it a few hundred yards, when sheets of rain pummeled down and the trail became slick and treacherous. I went slow or risk sliding and perhaps even going over the side. I stayed close to the hillside of the path and crept along, each step placed carefully.

By the time I exited the hiking trail, and was on resort property again, I was drenched. My clothes clung to me in a sodden mess, my shoes sloshed, and my hair was plastered to my head. Embarrassed to enter and leave a trail of water everywhere I went, I jogged up to the back deck where the smoker's section was and ducked through the side door. At least I wasn't sticky hot any more.

I sloshed to the lobby and returned the binoculars to the desk clerk, who smiled and told me not to worry about my trailing water. Blair was just returning from her makeover at the spa and stopped when she saw me. Her hair was shoulder length and cut in a cute bob with some highlights added that made her look young and her nails had a nice French manicure.

"Oh, my! How did you get so wet?"

"I went on a nice hike back there. I was so busy using the binoculars that I was taken by surprise when the clouds blocked out the sun and the downpour began." There, no hint that I was trying to follow the trail of the killer. *Nope, I'm innocent and have no idea where the murderer would have escaped or what route.* I just hoped I was believable.

"You need to go dry off. I hope those shoes will survive the experience."

"When is your hot date?" I teased.

"In forty-five minutes. I'm going to put some makeup on and get dressed. Wish me luck." She smiled and looked so happy.

"Best of luck, dear." And I meant it.

In my room, I showered and then hung my wet clothes over the shower rod to dry. By that time, Mason was back from his day and it was his turn in the shower.

While Mason showered, I phoned Detective Sullivan.

"Hello Detective, miss me?" I chimed when he answered.

He groaned, "Miss LaMere. Now you are calling me, too? Better make this quick or people will start to talk." His voice remained official, but he was cracking a joke, wasn't he?

"Yes, sir. I spent the afternoon on that hiking trail behind the resort. It has a vantage point where the killer could have shot from and the trail is really the most logical route to hide the weapon and maybe even change clothes before slipping down and leaving via a car in the lot or return to a guest room with nobody the wiser. I had to stop looking because of the rain dumping on me, but I'll walk the trail tomorrow morning again."

"Oh, joy! Yes, we know about the vantage point, but that would take a miraculous shot from over one hundred yards and there are only a few people in the world who could pull it off. We checked, they were all busy." He was just sounding condescending now.

I sighed, "Oh, so you already looked the trail over?" I felt a little stupid. Of course they had.

"Otherwise, I agree. That trail is the most likely

escape route, but it was dark and even in the moonlight I don't know many people who would attempt it. We didn't find anything, but you are welcome to walk that public trail all you want."

I hung up, feeling dejected. What about those boot prints I thought I saw? I would just have to go back in the morning and satisfy my curiosity on the public trail.

Mason joined me, dressed for dinner in grey slacks and a baby-blue button-down shirt that made his eyes seem more cobalt blue. "Marisa is leaving in the morning, I thought we could go out for dinner together if that's good for you?"

I had wanted to get through all the research tonight, but I know Mason was more upset about his father's interference using Tiffany than he let on, and I was grateful for Marisa's intervention. Besides, it would be good to just relax a little after the warning note and getting drenched in the rain.

I put on a more formal blue with white leafy fronds print sleeveless summer dress with a full skirt at knee length I paired with white strappy shoes. We met Marisa in the lobby and I was just in time to witness Whittaker Tate escorting Blair to his Mercedes at the curb. She looked lovely in a flowing Salmon chiffon dress with a matching chiffon shawl. Blair seemed to have blossomed in a few short days, like she was working through her grief and living again.

Marisa dressed in a white halter dress with a white bangle bracelet and matching earrings. She looked like she was a runway model. I was definitely feeling the pressure between Marisa's fashion sense and cousin Felicia's pushing me to dress more stylish. Marisa took my arm like we were family already and walked with me to the car. Mason had made reservations at Cochise restaurant, a gourmet chic eatery. I just hoped I didn't drop something or use the wrong fork.

We were seated in a beautiful adobe house built in 1756 with kiva fireplaces, wood beams, leather seats, and white linen tablecloths. The walls had large stunning paintings of horses and the lighting was from antler chandeliers. We ordered our preferred wines, perused the menu and ended up with jumbo Maine crab cakes for an appetizer, I ordered the sea bass, Marisa the fiery sweet chile & honey-grilled prawns, and Mason the mesquite grilled Maine lobster tails with angel hair pasta.

As soon as our orders were in, Marisa wasted no time. "So what was this about a dead body left at your door the night before last? Didn't I hear about some venture capitalist already killed there?"

Mason and I looked at each other. We should have known she would circle around to that before too long. I am surprised she didn't bring it up at breakfast this morning. This gave us something to talk about besides the awkward issue of their father sabotaging my relationship with Mason.

I began in a quiet voice so other diners didn't hear, "Maybe I should start at the beginning. The evening we arrived we were strolling in the moonlight and Merritt Howell grabbed my ankle as he was dying and said *the curse got him...*" Mason and I tag teamed telling the whole story.

Our food arrived and for the rest of the main course we talked about the food, Marisa's new job, and enjoyed the time together. Over caramel crème brûlée desert and decaf coffee all around, I shared what I found out about the big game archery equipment used, and my hiking expedition that I wanted to continue in the morning. I withheld the threatening note left resting on my person after my massage, which still gave me the heebie jeebies when I thought about it. They didn't need to worry about something none of us could do anything about.

Marisa had gotten really into the slate of suspects and the maze of motives, "But you haven't really looked over the scene of the second murder, even though it was at your door. Maybe when we get back we should look that over as well?"

Mason shook his head, "I'm so glad I don't have to worry about you two getting along. If anything, I don't know who will be the most corrupting influence on the other." We laughed and toasted to that.

Marisa called a server over and enlisted her to take a group photo on each of our cell phones. It felt more like a party than a simple dinner, and I could tell Marisa was trying extra hard to make up for the Tiffany debacle, which made me like her even more.

On the drive back to the resort, Marisa brought it up again. "So, we'll look over the second murder site just outside your door. How close can a bow effectively shoot?"

Mason jumped in, replying, "Archery practice can be as close as five feet from the target. I wouldn't think any closer than ten feet in our situation because the victim could knock it out of the shooter's hands or other tactics."

"So a long hallway would work." Marisa stated.

A shiver ran down my spine. How many times did I enter a hallway without a second thought, caught up in my own thoughts? Preston could have strode into that hallway with his head in his own thoughts and not even noticed the shooter waiting at the other end until it was too late. That was sobering. I didn't know if Preston's guest room was on that floor, or if he was on his way somewhere. What if Preston, like Merritt, had received text messages?

I had seen Merritt at dinner, texting back and forth.

I remember wondering the night he was killed if he had received a text to meet for a liaison off-the-path in the garden to only find a killer waiting. But the same tactic could have worked on Preston. Text him to come to a room for a meeting or chat, only to find the killer waiting to shoot him the moment he walked into the hallway.

I hadn't thought about that detail to tell Detective Sullivan, drat. But surely they had each victim's cell phone and could see any texts and find who sent them, right?

Mason cut through my thoughts, "We can look, but the forensics team went over the entire hallway, I doubt we'll discover anything new."

I had to keep this low key, "I've gone back to a subtle approach at the resort, so we need to make this look innocent to other guests. Not like we're investigating." My voice stayed calm and level, at least to my ears.

"Oh, that's a bit after the fact." He looked at me with a side glance that made it clear he thought there was more to it. I looked out the window.

When we arrived back at Enchantment Canyon, Marisa followed us up to our room. She wouldn't let it go. I stood next to our door and Mason walked down a few paces and raised his arms as if he had a bow and arrow. The sight was chilling. He looked around at the other doors to each side, then stepped back to the end of the hall and looked around. He disappeared, and I heard the door to the stairway close. Marisa ran after him. They were gone for about a minute.

I was left in the hallway where a man had been killed in this spot. I took my key card and ducked into my room; I wasn't standing out there any longer. Although I kept my door cracked and looked outside every few seconds until I saw Mason and Marisa return and waved to them.

They joined me in the room and Marisa couldn't contain herself, "That has to be it. The killer stood at the end of the hallway so a guest didn't open the door and expose him. Then exited into the stairs. That goes down to an outside exit door, and from there disappeared." She was a bit too excited about the discovery. Was I rubbing off on her?

"I'm sure the police have been over it with their forensics." Mason said as he looked at me.

"Yes, they probably did." I agreed. Detective Sullivan would have figured it out like we did. It made sense. It was easy for the killer to make their way to the hiking trail and disappear again. I was convinced even more now that somewhere along that hiking trail the murder weapon was hidden where it could easily be accessed. Even if the killer were Yates or Whittaker, they could drive here and park in the lot, make their way unseen to the trail where they gathered the weapon and after committing murder, hide it again, and find their way to their car. So long as they weren't seen with the weapon, nobody would think twice about their presence. And like this afternoon, I was sure they had a change of dark clothes hidden as well. This was premeditated and cold-blooded, not spontaneous. I had to be discreet tomorrow on the trail. The earlier I left, the better chance I wouldn't be observed.

Marisa seemed reluctant to end the evening, so Mason suggested we have a nightcap in the lounge.

"I didn't think they encouraged alcohol with the health and wellness emphasis?" Marisa said.

Mason winked, "They don't, but I bring my own stock. If one of you wouldn't mind smuggling a few sample size bottles in your purses, we'll be set."

A nightcap was fine by me. Not only would I get more time with Marisa, but anyone watching would think that I wasn't pursuing the murders any further. We spent another hour with Marisa before Mason and I both succumbed to enormous yawns. After goodbyes, in which Marisa gave a round of bear hugs, she reluctantly let us go.

I took my laptop to bed with me and began reading through the material Beverly had sent, again. I faded into sleep after only ten minutes and dreamed the rest of the night of a hidden killer shooting deadly arrows from behind palm trees or bushes.

Mason woke me with a gentle kiss before sunrise for his last day of photography. Rather than go back to sleep, I fought to wake up and be ready for the hiking trail when the sun came up. The laptop had fallen to the floor in the night. I picked it up to put away and had the nagging feeling I needed to read it. Maybe when I get back from the hike, I could devote time to it without succumbing to sleep again, but not now.

I was ready for my hike a little before sunrise and made my way to the little cafe for a cappuccino and something to eat that I could take along. They didn't have any portable foods like granola bars, so I grabbed a smoothie before I left. It would have to do.

I was just a few hundred feet into the trail when I stopped to watch bright salmon and violet colors splash the sky in splendor. I enjoyed my smoothie while I reveled in the colors. Now I understood why New Mexico was called the land of enchantment. It was more than a regular sunrise, the energy in the air was charged.

I watched until the colors faded and pushed forward on the trail. I wanted to get my search-and-find mission done before the temperatures reached over a hundred like yesterday. I kept an eye out for snakes and tarantulas, my personal fear, along with any sign of boot prints or places to hide.

I passed the scraggly tree I took shelter under yesterday. The temperature was rising already. I stopped to drink from my bottled water and use the front desk's binoculars to study my surroundings. Nothing of note yet, but at least I wasn't imagining boot prints mysteriously ahead. I continued on, my legs now tired. I spotted a section of the trail with an over-hang providing shade and stopped there. It appeared as though water and the elements had eroded a section of the rocky hill. I wasn't tall, but I still had to stoop slightly to stay in the shade.

I drank some more water and took my binoculars to look around again. I lowered the binoculars. Up the trail a few hundred feet, a man in traditional Native American buckskins pointing in my direction. I raised the binoculars. He wasn't there. I shook my head to clear it. Maybe just knowing I was in the location of the legendary Indian brave caused my imagination to conjure him.

I looked around at what he could have been pointing to and only saw some boulders littering the ground under the overhang. I looked up the path and there he was again. From this distance he looked like a rough life had made him grizzled. He seemed big from my vantage point, broad shouldered, and a look in his eyes that scared me. He pointed again with urgency, not exactly directly at me but… under the overhang.

I crouched and hobbled further under the outcropping. Behind a boulder, I spotted the edge of a tan canvas tarp. I scrambled over the rocks in my way, and slowly lifted the tarp, half afraid of what I would find. There was what I had been looking for, a large black contraption that only resembled the ancient bow in the string strung to propel an arrow. Otherwise it looked like a sci-fi version, with the tips holding little wheels that the string looped through a few times and criss-crossed from what I could see. Next to that was a canvas quiver holding a handful of lethal looking arrows.

I dropped the end of the tarp and made my way out from under the overhang. Fortunately, my cell phone had a few bars showing, so I called Detective Sullivan. I waited for several minutes before he finally took me off hold.

"Miss LaMere, this is getting old…"

"I found the murder weapon, you need to hurry." I cut him off.

"What? Where are you?" He demanded.

I explained roughly where I was on the trail and what I saw hidden. "I don't want to be standing around waiting for you guys and the killer show up. Do you think you can hurry, please? Oh, and don't make a big scene at the resort and scare off the killer." I rushed to get out. Now that I had found the evidence, I was antsy to be far away from it.

"Let me worry about that. I'll be there shortly. Hide as best you can until you hear me call for you."

I looked around again for a hiding place, but there weren't any options. Then I saw the vision of the Indian brave again further up the trail, motioning his arm for me to follow and he walked off. *What did I have to lose?* I trotted up the trail until I saw him pointing up the hillside about six feet to a hollow or a cave opening. He vanished in the blink of an eye.

I didn't think twice, but searched for handholds and climbed up the short distance. I had to leverage myself to swing a leg up and over. Once I was up, I could see the hiding place. I ducked into a cave and realized this was where the old bow and arrow were reportedly found.

"Don't mind me, just going to hang out here for a few moments. I won't disturb anything, I promise." I said into the dark recesses that stretched back. I listened, half expecting the murderer to emerge and kill me. It was eerily quiet and still. I stayed to the side of the entrance in the shadows and waited to hear Detective Sullivan call my name. Every bird call or unidentifiable noise made me jump. I used my cell phone flashlight when I swore I heard a snake slithering near me in the dirt, but there was nothing. I checked my cell phone, it was nearly thirty minutes since I had called the detective, but it seemed like hours to me. I sat down on the dirt floor, afraid to leave the shadows.

Eventually, I heard voices. They weren't even trying to be quiet as they came closer. Finally, I heard Detective Sullivan call out my name.

I yelled out and deserted my hiding place. Behind me I heard a whisper: *My vengeance has been served on all three.*

CHAPTER 16

The hair on the back of my neck and my arms stood up. I scurried down the six feet of terrain with no regard for scrapes or bruises. I was caked in dirt, but I didn't care so long as I was away from the creepy whisper in the cave.

I jogged up to Detective Sullivan, and he looked me up and down, "What happened to you?"

"I hid in a cave up there." I pointed.

"You look scared. Did something happen?"

"Nope, nothing." I wasn't sharing my paranoid imaginings. I brushed off layers of dirt and hoped on one foot as I emptied my shoes of soil.

I watched as the forensics team carefully bagged and tagged everything, including the tarp.

"Detective, I touched the tarp to lift it. So my prints will be on it." I said with some concern in my voice.

"No problem. I'm hoping we have the killer's prints on the equipment there." He said.

They marched the evidence bags containing the bow and arrows past me. The bow looked even more futuristic as it passed. It didn't look that much like any bow I'd ever seen.

"Is that really a bow, it looks so strange, like something from a space movie?" I asked.

"Oh yes, that is a compound bow and they are very advanced."

Forensics was going over every rock in the overhang, looking for anything more left behind.

"I guess I'll go back to Enchantment Canyon now. Tell me you were subtle coming to retrieve this."

"Don't worry, we have a few tricks up our sleeves. Are you going to stop poking around now? You've done enough. I'll call Carlos and ask him to inform your boss you helped locate the murder weapon. Just lie low now."

I nodded my head. I wasn't fully listening.

One of the forensic technicians called out and held up another evidence bag, a small one this time. As they carried them past me, I saw it was a cell phone with something else in the bag.

The tech stopped and let the detective look it over in the bag, Sullivan handed it back.

"What was that?" I might as well get as much as I can from the situation.

"That would be a cell phone with what appears to be a solar charger." He commented.

"I suspected the killer lured the victims to locations that were advantageous for shooting them. At dinner that night, I noticed Merritt texting a lot." I said as casually as possible.

He stared at me.

"it occurred to me after my visit with you yesterday. I was going to tell you and then I found this." I explained. "Did you find any clothes?"

"No, were you expecting some?"

"I speculated with Merritt's murder the killer could've been wearing dark clothes to go unseen, and I just figured the clothes would be stashed with the weapon."

He looked at me for a while before speaking again. "Can you make it back all right or do you need an escort?"

I had been dismissed. "I'm fine. I don't need a chaperone."

I picked my way through the crowd of forensics techs and police officers.

By the time I made it back to Enchantment Canyon, I was hot and grimy. I had drained my water bottle and felt parched. After a shower, I discovered multiple scrapes and bruises from my little adventure, but none anywhere visible like my face. I was famished, so I went to the cafe for brunch.

The hostess seated me in a corner, which gave a perfect view of the tables and diners. I placed my order for two eggs, whole wheat pancakes, turkey bacon and another coffee. Blair was a few tables away with her back to me, but I wasn't in the mood for company, all things considered. I hoped she had a good time on her date. Maybe I would stop on my way out and ask.

I thought over the discovery of the weapon and cell phone. I ignored the mysterious voice in the cave and the boot prints leading me to the spot. There was no need to think of it again, I clearly had imagined them. How long would it take to identify any fingerprints? Not fast enough, I figured.

I was no closer to pinpointing who the killer was or why, and most of the Howell Venture people were leaving this afternoon after their wrap-up session. Yates Aldrich and Whittaker Tate could have already left their hotels this morning. The suspects were scattering to the four winds, and I had failed. Sure, it wasn't really my job; I got that. Even so, it seemed like I was so close to unveiling the killer.

I finished my breakfast and downed plenty of water to rehydrate. I stopped to say hello to Blair on my way out.

"Hello there, I won't stay long. I just wanted to ask how your evening went last night? I hope you had a great time." Her hair was not as full of body as after the makeover, but otherwise she looked content and she beamed at my inquiry.

She dabbed at her mouth with a linen napkin, "Thank you, dear. You've been so kind to me. I truly appreciate that." She took a drink of orange juice before continuing, "Mr Tate was delightful. We had a lovely dinner, and he kept me laughing with stories. I felt special, and it's been a long time since I've felt that. That was an unexpected memory I'll treasure."

The way she talked it sounded like she wasn't expecting to live long, and once again I wondered about her health. Or she was still grieving the loss of her husband. I know everybody handles grief differently. My father was depressed for a long while after my mother died from Breast Cancer. After six months, he nearly smothered me with attention, as if he had to pour all of himself into me to keep his sanity.

"Any chance you'll see each other again?" I was getting sentimental. *When did that happen?*

"Oh, I doubt it very much. But it was nice for an evening." She had a faraway look in her eyes. My heart ached for her.

"Maybe you can go out again tonight?" I didn't feel

bad fishing for information on when Tate might leave, since he was my top suspect.

"He didn't ask and I don't feel right asking him. That seems so needy." She smiled shyly.

"Well, he should snatch you up, you're a catch." Her blush deepened.

We chatted for another minute before I made my way to the offices. Audrey ushered me into Jonathon's office and Carlos joined us with Graciella and Maria.

I looked at all of them gathered, "What's going on?" I couldn't keep my suspicion that I had done something wrong from my voice.

Jonathan stood up, "We received word that you found the murder weapon. The detective hopes it'll contain fingerprints or DNA and solve the murders. We can't thank you enough." He pumped my hand mercilessly while the others pounded me on the back.

Audrey ushered in a platter of granola and yogurt parfaits, and we each grabbed one. They all looked at me as if I should give a speech. *Awkward.*

I cleared my throat, "Um, I couldn't have done it without each of your support and help. I just wish I could've figured out who the murder was before the suspects check out. This'll only be a minor blip for the resort and you'll continue to thrive and grow." Not too shabby for an impromptu speech. I wasn't sure how accurate my words would prove to me, though.

My mouth was dry, and I felt warm, I was never very comfortable at speaking in front of people. I disliked everybody looking at me, witnessing every stammer or tongue-tied moment.

Graciella smiled and nodded, encouraging me.

"I only hope I trained you enough, since I'm supposed to leave in the morning."

Audrey chimed in, "You're better than you think. We've been doing the assignments you gave us a few times each and compared notes. I think we've gotten pretty familiar with the new system." Maria reassured me she felt confident enough to work with the other Customer Representatives on the system.

By the time the little party broke up, I had nothing to do but go to my room. I could finally go through the rest of the research from Beverly. But once I was in my room I felt anxious, I took my laptop and went to the lobby to camp out there as I scanned the articles and news items sent days ago. I had only breezed through a handful of the research since they were initially sent to me, and this seemed like the last vestiges of investigation that might give me a final resolution.

I sat in a chair where I could observe the rest of the lobby and started browsing through the multiple items Beverly had sent. There was a lot of information on Merritt Howell's hostile removal of Whittaker Tate, followed with the updates of Tate's wife's death. It was tragic. I could see how Merritt had pushed Tate beyond what he could bear. All for greed of power and money.

Eventually, I was deep into reading any mention of Howell's employees over the last few years in media or business blogs. There wasn't any revelation or ultimate piece that completed the picture. I got up and stretched a bit. After several days of being immersed in interviews or walking the trail, just sitting and reading was difficult. I was eager to finish and find who had killed two people.

I sure wasn't doing it because of any sense of duty to the two men, Merritt was deplorable. But I didn't want the killer getting away with murder. Time might pass, but locals would remember the murders at the resort and it could hurt their business. Revealing the motive and bringing the killer to justice would remove the stain on Enchantment Canyon Resort.

I hunkered back down to continue my research and fought to focus. Scanning through articles, I opened a link to a writeup about the winner of an archery competition. But it was a woman, and she wasn't a Howell employee. I almost closed the article and continued on until I noticed the woman's *husband* worked for the old Tate & Howell Venture Capital. This employee, whose wife was into competitive archery, was a name I didn't recognize.

I opened up a search engine and looked for this

employee. I finally found an article praising his savvy approach to identifying startup companies to invest in that were paying off in large returns. This man was making the company a lot of money. I finally found a mention that he had left the company because of being diagnosed with cancer.

I sat looking off as pieces snapped into place. Tate knew this employee, and probably the wife, since that was before he was pushed out. I suspected he thought of something or someone during the second interview in the guest library, but I couldn't force it out of him.

I couldn't find any other mentions of this man online. I returned to the original archery article. *Could it be?* The woman in the photo only slightly seemed familiar, like a vague sense of Deja Vu you get.

I looked up and saw Blair rolling her luggage out the door to leave. She looked at me, and in that moment we both knew. She was an archery champion. But why would she kill two men? She hustled out of the door, her keys in her hand. She was about to get away, and she would run and hide now that I knew. How close to Mexico was it from here?

Mason had the vehicle we drove here in. I ran to Audrey's office, threw my laptop down, and asked for the resort vehicle like I did yesterday. She looked at me and didn't ask why, just handed me the keys. As I ran out, I heard her on the phone with Carlos.

I didn't have my purse or my license with me, but I wouldn't waste time retrieving them from my room. I raced across the lobby, threw the doors open, and sprinted to the nearby SUV. I glimpsed of Blair's car turning away from town, so I followed, hoping to catch up to her. I leaned forward enough to get my cell phone from my back pocket. One handed I called Detective Sullivan, but was told he wasn't in the office. Crap, he probably was still on the trail as they looked for more evidence.

"You don't understand, I'm in pursuit of the double murderer. Can't you patch me through to him or something?"

"No, but if you give me your location, I'll let him know. Or, I can have him call you."

"You'll be out of a job if the killer gets away because you won't take me seriously. I found the danged murder weapon this morning, and now I'm following the killer. If she gets away, or I am injured, it's on your head." I hung up, completely frustrated.

I focused on my driving. It was a two-lane road leading further into the desert, but at least it was paved. I saw Blair's gray older model sedan a mile or more ahead of me on the straightaway. Then it dipped down out of sight as the road went into a valley. I was driving without a license, but I figured a speeding ticket was a risk I would take.

As I zoomed along over the speed limit, I wondered why sad and grieving Blair would have killed two men. I just couldn't understand it, but I was sure it was Blair. I didn't have all the information. Could grieving cause her to lose perspective and blame them for her husband's death somehow?

I reached the spot where her car had dipped out of sight just in time to see it crest a slight hill ahead and vanish from sight again. Maybe I was far enough back that she didn't realize I was following her. But I was lost, I had no clue where I was and that made me uncomfortable.

My cell phone rang, "Hello."

"Miss LaMere, what in the blazes are you doing? I got a call from Carlos and then a sergeant at the precinct claiming you threatened him." He yelled.

"I'm following the murderer, thought you might be interested to know who it is and where to find her? But your sergeant told me to wait until you got around to calling me back." I didn't bother keeping the sarcasm from my voice.

"You know who the killer is? Who?"

"There was a guest at the resort named Blair Palmer. She's a world class archery champion, and oh by-the-way she was married to a former Howell executive. She's running for it and I am in pursuit." I spoke so fast, I hoped he could separate the words and understand.

I reached the top of the next rise and saw her vehicle far in the distance turning off the road. I also saw a state road sign.

I relayed the small state road I was on, my direction, and the mile marker I just passed. "But she turned off up ahead. I don't know what that road is."

"I know it. I'm on my way. There is nothing out there. Will you pull off and let us follow her?"

"She'll get away before you even get close. Just get here fast."

"Be careful…" was all he got out before my phone connection dropped.

I tossed my cell phone in the passenger seat. Well, here I go chasing a killer. What was I thinking? I resolved to not get close to her, I was just going to report her location, not try and interfere. I would stay safe.

I finally reached the turn off and followed, but I had lost sight of Blair. I squinted looking into the distance. I kept my speed up and as I zoomed along. I looked from left to right for any sign of her. I didn't want to miss her if she knew a little cattle track or something.

Crap. Why didn't I see the clues? She didn't like talking about her husband or her life. But then I didn't share my life, either. Tthere had to have been signs, something. Perhaps after the threatening note, my thinking the killer didn't really want to hurt me was the biggest clue. Blair had found me locked in the Sauna, as if she didn't want me too scared. I noticed her fingers were callused, were they from archery? When I was checking in, Blair glared at Merritt. It was a brief moment as I walked up the stairs, but she had definitely scowled at him. The night of Merritt's murder, she had joined the crowd watching the police, and she was dressed in black.

Over the drone of the tires on the pavement and the air conditioning I heard a noise. I looked all around. When I leaned forward and looked up I saw a helicopter overhead, but it was private, not police. The only reason for a helicopter out here was for a rancher managing a herd, which I had seen no evidence of any livestock. Or the obvious, to pick somebody up secretly. How was Blair capable of such a luxury to escape?

It was ridiculous, but could she be a hired assassin with her archery skills? No, that was ludicrous. She wouldn't have hesitated to hurt me if that were truly the case. No, that couldn't be it. Then how did she manage such a getaway?

Whittaker Tate! He must have recognized her, that's why he took her out to dinner. This had to be his rescuing her and whisking her away, since she did what he couldn't bring himself to do. That was logical. I think. It wasn't far fetched at least.

The helicopter veered to the left. Out in the middle of the barron landscape I could see Blair's car. I almost missed the dirt road, not much more than a horse trail, that came up suddenly. I slid into the curve and my stomach clenched and twisted as the SUV veered off the dirt road and bounced over a few yucca plants before getting back onto the hard packed dirt of the road.

The helicopter was landing, churning up a dust storm that enveloped it and Blair's car. The rotors slowed and finally stopped. I saw a man running from the helicopter to the car and grab luggage.

I started honking, long and loud. The man looked up and then ran with the luggage. It could be Tate, but I wasn't positive. Blair ran after him. He threw the luggage into the back of the copter and ran around to jump into the pilot seat. Blair climbed into the passenger seat.

I was gaining on them, but would never get there to get a tail number. I wish I had the cheapo little binoculars the resort leant out.

The blades were starting up again when a police helicopter roared past overhead, and hovered in front of the getaway chopper. The police helicopter's side door slid back, and a sniper with a rifle leaned out. The message was clear, don't even think about taking off. The getaway pilot raised his hands and the whirling blades slowed.

A few minutes later, I was parked a few hundred yards away, just in case any shooting started. Detective Sullivan exited the police copter once it landed and the dust cloud settled. He reached me and socked me in the arm.

"Woman, you scared the crap out of me," Then we high fived.

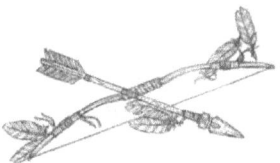

CHAPTER 17

J insisted on going to the police station. I couldn't stand not knowing why sad and grieving Blair would kill two people.

When I got cell phone reception again, I called Audrey to let her know the killer was caught and to make sure Mason knew I was following up on the arrest and would be at the police station.

I vowed to spring for a car wash before bringing the SUV back. I had to resist writing on the dirt encrusted back window *Wash Me.* Inside the station, I was immediately directed back to the small little closet sized interrogation rooms. It was nothing like on television where they are dramatic sets, these were just claustrophobic with hard chairs. I was waved into an adjoining room where a television was set up showing the room next door.

Blair sat alone in the room and looked resigned to her fate. After several minutes, Detective Sullivan finally walked into the room. I anticipated this taking a long time, but Blair didn't even ask for a lawyer.

"Does this mean you're ready to tell us what happened?" Detective Sullivan asked.

"I wish to make a statement." She sat up straighter and threw her shoulders back, "I felt that Merritt Howell contributed to the death of my husband. He had to pay for the pain and suffering he caused." She said in a clear, strong voice.

"But I thought your husband died of cancer." He shot back.

"He was considered on sick leave for the first few months so he was covered by his usual insurance. We found out very quickly that the insurance coverage we had as his company benefit had been downgraded as part of Merritt's cost cutting measures. We quickly ran out of money to subsidize the treatments. I sent letters pleading that Merritt simply upgrade the insurance to the level we had before, so we could afford his treatments. He refused. Then Merritt gave an ultimatum that he couldn't be on sick leave forever, he had to either come back to work or be let go. He could've laid him off, so we had severance pay, but he just fired him. We lost the house, all his stocks, everything." The more she spoke, the angrier she got. I was getting angry myself.

"After he fired my husband, we tried to buy supplemental insurance, but couldn't afford the cost they required because he was in the middle of battling cancer. We ended up in a tiny one bedroom apartment, and nothing more we could sell, pawn, or scrape together for treatments. He died a horrible death of pain and suffering. " She took a shaky breath, as if the recounting of the story would bring her to tears.

"That was bad enough. Then I found out that he still had the key man insurance on my husband, and received well over ten million dollars when my husband died. I was destitute, sleeping on a friend's couch. I had to do a crowdfunding campaign to bury my husband. I went to the offices and pleaded with Merritt to pay for the funeral with that insurance payout, it wouldn't hurt them. He laughed in my face. Said we should've saved our money better. I should pull myself up by my bootstraps." Her face turned hard as granite.

"I'm dying. Because every dime went to my husband for his treatments, we couldn't even afford vitamins for me. So, I did a crowdfunding campaign to raise money for my dying wish, one last hurrah. I planned to come here during their annual meeting and kill Merritt, then kill myself. Trying to save his own hide, Merritt confessed

Preston was the numbers guy and he identified the cost cutting measures and maintained the key man insurance. He wasn't laughing when I put that handmade arrow in him. I changed my plans to kill Preston and then leave here and end my suffering." She bowed her head and folded her hands in her lap. Tears rolled down her cheeks.

I wiped away my tears. Detective Sullivan tried to ask some more questions, but she wasn't saying anything more. After a few moments, he joined me in the observation room. He stood next to me for a few moments without speaking.

Eventually I managed, "I wish I hadn't figured it out. She has already paid enough." My tears dripped down my face again.

"I know, but we don't get to decide that. If she's sick and dying, she'll at least have regular food and medical care while in custody." We stood there watching Blair on the monitor as she silently cried.

I turned because I couldn't watch anymore. "What did Tate say?"

"He recognized her and knew she was a world class competitive archer. He made a few calls before their date and found out her grief was as bad as his, if not worse. He was going to take her to a private hospital to live out the rest of her life. At least, that's what he claims."

Detective Sullivan escorted me out of the observation room. I sat at his desk, staring off into space for a long time while he continued working on the case. I could blame myself for getting involved, but it was all water under the bridge. I had really liked her and felt for her.

After a while, I realized Mason was standing next to me. He wrapped me in his arms and we just stood in the middle of the squad room holding each other. My sorrow over the entire mess bubbled up, and I cried. We went back to the resort and sat in the hot tub with spiked drinks. I told Mason everything, even being locked in the Sauna and the note left on me at the spa. He didn't say anything, probably afraid I would cry. But I was all done crying for now.

After the hot tub, he let me sleep for a little bit in the room. When I woke up I felt better. I still ached for Blair and everything she had gone through, but I couldn't change a thing. I couldn't blame myself for revealing she was the killer. Even though Merritt was reprehensible, I lived in a country with the rule of law, and she had broken it. There were consequences for every action.

Mason and I dressed for dinner and I put a smile on like makeup. I might not feel like it, but I would have a genuine smile again someday. During dinner, we chatted about anything and everything, except Blair.

"I have a couple of surprises for you." Mason said

mid way through our meal, "First, we get to stay here for a few days just to relax, compliments of your boss." He took a deep breath, "And I've arranged for Detective Sullivan to tell you where you can write Blair. I think that would be good for both of you."

"Thank you." I smiled half heartedly, "Now I would like to dance in the lounge, and act like none of this happened for a while, and have you kiss me and sweep me off my feet."

Tonight the "do not disturb" sign was going on our door, because life was just too short.

The Gran Paloma (Paloma=Spanish for "dove)

This is my own version of the refreshing Paloma cocktail that isn't strong on the liquor. Paloma is practically the national cocktail in Mexico, so it seemed perfect to introduce while Julienne visits New Mexico (which is in the U.S.) Traditionally, you drink it in clay mugs (called Jarritos de Barro) that keep it cold. The mugs come in a simple glaze or brightly painted.

Ingredients

1 oz Tequila (Blanco or lightly aged reposado is best)

1 oz Gran Marnier

1 oz Fresh grapefruit juice (or more to taste)

Squirt soda

Grapefruit wedge for garnish

Tejin for rim
Paloma clay mugs, or highball glass

Directions

1. Wet the rim with a grapefruit wedge, then dip or roll in Tejin.
2. Add about half a glass of ice.
3. Put Tequila, Gran Marnier, and grapefruit juice in a drink shaker, cap and shake. If you don't have a shaker, mix directly in the glass.
4. Pour into Paloma clay mugs (or what you have available) over the ice.
5. Top off with Squirt soda.
6. Place a grapefruit wedge on the rim for garnish.

THANK YOU FOR READING!

Dear Reader,

I hope you enjoyed ARROWED: Resort to Murder Mystery IV. I really enjoyed writing the characters and the locations! I hope Julienne's adventures entertained you, and you are looking forward to the next book, STONED.

Finally, I need to ask you a favor. If you're so inclined, I'd love a review of ARROWED. Whether you loved it or hated it - I'd just enjoy your feedback. Reviews can be tough to come by these days. You, the reader, have the power to make or break a book.

Also, feel free to contact me at mysterysuspense1@gmail.com if you have spotted any typos that have escaped my editor and proofreader's attention. Let me know where you found the typos or errors.

Subscribe to my newsletter for exclusive content and specials: http://eepurl.com/c2DgfT

Thank you for reading ARROWED and spending time with me. The next book in the series will be STONED and it will take place in the North East U.S.

In gratitude,
Avery Daniels

ABOUT THE AUTHOR

Avery Daniels was born and raised in Colorado, graduated from college with a degree in business administration, and has worked in fortune 500 companies and Department of Defense her entire life. Her most eventful job was apartment management for 352 units. She still resides in Colorado with two brother black cats as her spirited companions. She volunteers for a cat shelter, enjoys scrapbooking and card making, photography, and painting in watercolor and acrylic. She inherited a love for reading from her mother and grandmother and grew up talking about books at the dinner table.

Let's stay in touch.
Signup for exclusives and news :
http://eepurl.com/c2DgfT
Website: www.Avery-Daniels.com
Goodreads: www.goodreads.com/Avery-Daniels

Facebook: facebook.com/AveryDanielsAuthor
BookBub: www.bookbub.com/authors/avery-daniels

ALSO BY AVERY DANIELS

Iced

Nailed

Spiked

Arrowed

Coming: Stoned